NO LONGER
SHAARA OF SHAARVAN

Book Six of the Shaarvan Series

Note: To start at the beginning of this series, please go to
Scholar-Ship-Bound.

K.S. Riggin

Table of Contents

Main Characters & Places in the Shaarvan Series 1

Prelude 5

Chapter One 6

Chapter Two 58

Chapter Three 95

Chapter Four 146

Chapter Five... 189

Chapter Six 223

Chapter Seven 238

Main Characters & Places in the Shaarvan Series

Altar: Original home of the Shapechanger. It is both the name of a planet and the capital city.

Altarian: Those who live or were born on Altar.

Baltoff: The Old One on Westla who manufactured the drugs that Thenos used to overthrow the government of Altar.

Barquel: The main god worshipped on Freinana.

Blair: Owner of the Landoor ranch. Good guy.

Brala: Shaara's friend on Westla,

Chaslow: Shapechanger working for Thenos, blew up nursery on Westla & hunted for Shaara.

Clofa: One of Altar's two moons. It was where the old Shapechanger liked to retire. Thenos blew it up.

Crimson Black: The horse-like landoor Shaara befriends.

Flar: Freinana housemaster that Shaara stays with. Husband of Frieda.

Flaorth: A tracker implant which Shapechanger insert under the skin of females for identification purposes.

Frieda: Freinana housemistress that Shaara stays with. Wife of Flar.

Goria: Pseudo wife of Pathe. Former lover of Shaarvan. Bad person.

Isandor: The commoner who owns Shaara on Freinana. Bad guy.

Landoor: An animal that looks like a horse.

Mandar: A landoor the Guardians buy for Shaara on Westla.

Megloztar: Theinian slaver who kidnaps Shaara.

Parthrol: An Old One who lived on the former moon. He was thought to have known an antidote for what poisoned Tevor and the other Council members.

Pathe: Son of Tevor & Teea (brother of Shaarvan & Thenos.) Doctor, good guy.

Saberey: Symbol of the Shapechanger & their origin

Shaara: College student. Wife of Shaarvan and later Stegthal (Thal) Renamed numerous times: Susan, Sletttha, Sleena, Skeva, Thalia, Thenosa.

Shaarac: (**Thaarac**, **Thenon**) Shaara and Shaarvan's son.

Shaarvan: Steals his wife, Shaara, from a college campus, Altarian Shapechanger.

Shaandar: (Thandar, Thenor) second son of Shaara and Shaarvan. (Biological son of Thal and Thalia) He was claimed by Tenos and proclaimed the royal heir, so he is officially Prince Thenor.)

Spelon: One of Shaara's guardians. Shapechanger Warrior.

Starna: Formerly Teea, but since Starnkor is her new husband, she was renamed.

Starnkor: Teea's Second Husband.

Stegthal: (**Thal**) He becomes Shaara's Second Husband. He was killed on Westla, defending Shaara. Good & bad.

Stubra: The small goat-donkey animal found on Deathstar. They were mostly used to carry loads but were friendly creatures that Shaara and Shaarac treated as pets.

Susan: Shaara's original Earth name.

Targone: Shapechanger who arrives on Freinana to verify that Shaara is Shapechanger.

Teea: Shaarvan's mother, lives on Altar, wife of Tevor (and later Starnkor) She is renamed Starnka.

Tem: Head of Westla, Uncle to Shaarvan, Tevor's brother.

Temina: Wife of Tem, mentally unstable.

Tenor: One of Shaara's guardians. Shapechanger Warrior.

Tessa: High Priestess

Tevor: Shaarvan's father, lives on Altar, husband of Teea.

Thal: Stegthal's name on Deathstar.

Thaarac: (Shaarac) Son of Thalia and Shaarvan.

Thalia: Shaara's name on Deathstar.

Thandar: Shaara & Thal's son.

Thedar: One of Shaara's guardians. Shapechanger Warrior

Theinian: Males from a variety of planets, usually slavers and most often gay.

Thenos: Son of Tevor & Teea (brother of Shaarvan & Pathe.) Bad guy.

Tren: Owner of the casino and of Shaara. Good guy to Shaara.

Tura: Westlan Priestess who flies to Altar with Shaara.

Westla: Huge artificial satellite. Only Shapechanger may go there (other than the girls and servants that are brought to the planet.)

Additional Terminology:

Tide: Approximately an Earth day. Tides are usually grouped, as in a fiveTide, twentyTide, etc.

Pass: Approximately a year. A halfPass and quarterPass are common expressions.

Priestess: The rare female that can pass to test ten. Priestesses are honored and given extra rights.

Shapechanger: Never found in the plural. The Shapechanger are an artificially derived species that are capable of shape change, most often as a Saberey (tiger-like cat), Shapechanger also possess many sensory improvements and abilities.

The Names of Shapechanger: Names beginning with T or S denote Power. Those Shapechanger are deemed Lords. Formal testing on Westla ranks them.

Warrior Shapechanger: Those who meet qualifications of specific battle readiness. Ranking is by formal tests on Westla.

Prelude

Years ago, I was a college student in Los Angeles. An interview for a scholarship brought me a one-way ticket into space. I'd fought my capture, but against my will, my husband altered, impregnated, and trained me to Shapechanger standards. I didn't accept many of the Shapechanger beliefs, but acceptance wasn't mandatory, while obedience was. My rocky Shapechanger transition, including a stay on Freinana where I'd been a slave, had mellowed my rebellions.

I loved Shaarvan and the son we'd created, but life is never placid. A war in his home world called to him. He left me with four huge Shapechanger Warriors, three of them guardians and one as my new husband. Forced to leave the massive artificial satellite called Westla, we'd journeyed to an inhabited planet for protection against Thenos, the new Altarian dictator. And now, still pining for my beloved husband Shaarvan but bound to Thal, I discover that I'm pregnant.

Chapter One

Thal

"You're pregnant." How difficult is that to say?

Some kind of warrior I am, afraid to tell a woman what has been done to her. I was sweating worse than if I had just worked out with Spelon. And why? Why was I afraid to tell her? Thalia has to accept it. She cannot change it. It was my right.

But she is delicate. And I love her. How un-Shapechanger to say. But is it not true that we cannot lie?

Her eyes were teary when she learned of the fact, but she didn't battle. Perhaps she's learning how to be an obedient Shapechanger wife, or else she's just in shock. But the important thing is she didn't reach for the snow.

On Westla, she came so close to dying. She has Power enough to make her wishes a reality, at least to choose to leave for the other Plane. Impregnating her made her body refuse death. It is a safety for our women (or for us, I suppose.)

Thalia was calm when I told her — calm for her. Is that a bad thing? Is it a sign that her rebellion is no more or only temporarily suppressed?

How would Shaarvan have handled this? Would he have known gentler words? But does it matter? She loved Shaarvan. She would have accepted his child. No. Be honest. She loves Shaarvan *still*. I assume he still lives.

He and I discussed this. Shaarvan said it was a possibility he would be away for a long while. Perhaps he knew he would be caught up in the war. And the length of any war is never short.

It was almost the last thing he said to me. "If I do not return, she must bear at least two other children. Westla has mandated it, so do what needs to be done. After all, you will make an excellent father," he'd told me.

Will I be a good father? Despite my years, I have no practice at it. A baby has needs. A father must be patient when the boy crawls about and drools over important books.

I have been uncomplaining with Thaarac. I have told him stories and jiggled him about on my lap. He will be good practice for a baby, and the others will assist. They are good with Thaarac, so they will be good with . . . Thandar. I shall call him Thandar.

Raised by bachelors and a girl child. Poor child — children, since Thaarac may not even remember any other father than me. A child's memory is short.

But we will do all right. The baby will be fine, and Thaarac will continue to be happy, knowing no other way. It is Thalia I must be patient with. Can I be what she needs?

Thalia

In all the days that we had been on Deadstar, we had never seen a single dangerous animal. My heavy guards had slowly been dropped, and I'd been given the freedom to walk about. Taking advantage of it, I picked up Thaarac and went to find my guardians.

Of course, I knew there was not a single thing they could do about my being pregnant. I figured they'd probably be on Thal's side. I wished Brala were nearby. I'd love to have a woman-talking session.

But males were all I had. They'd have to do.

Thaarac's loud screams announced our coming. He wasn't hurt; he was just testing the air currents. He was always making sounds now. Screaming was his latest joy, especially since it usually brought people running.

My bondmates were working on our newest building, a kind of storage shed, I think.

"I need to talk to you," I said to them all, but I think I meant Thedar.

Thedar was sometimes my favorite — well, he and Tenor. The two of them comforted me more than disciplined. I think they actually liked me. Not because I belonged to Shaarvan or to Stegthal, but because they took the time to get to know me. Thedar told me once that I was clever and a quick learner. Tenor just smiled at me a lot. Sometimes, that's all you need to feel good about a person.

I couldn't say the same for Spelon. He was always gruff and ready to put me in my place for being smaller, weaker, unskilled, and, in general, not worth much. Or at least that's how he made me feel.

Tenor was like a father figure. He laughed with me, not at me. And Thedar, dear Thedar, He was my confidant if there were such a thing among big, strong Shapechanger males.

"You want to talk?" Spelon said, rolling his eyes. "I thought that you came to give us a hand. Perhaps you could lift up a couple of boulders for the . . ."

"Let her be," Thedar interrupted, butting Spelon in the hips. "It sounds like a crisis," Thedar added, teasing me.

Tenor reached out his hands for Thaarac, who was trying to wiggle out of my hold.

"Te," Thaarac cried out as I handed him over. Thaarac loved all the Shapechanger lords, but he changed favorites daily.

For a moment, I watched my son, hanging backward over Tenor's legs, giggling with pleasure.

I loved Thaarac so much that it hurt sometimes. He was my little golden wonder. Already, he had the look of Shaarvan in the color of his hair and in the planes of his chubby little face. His smile, with his tiny, little baby teeth, shouldn't remind me of Shaarvan. How could it? Yet it did. No matter how I tried to find the similarity, I couldn't, but Thaarac smiled just like his father, dimples and all.

Thedar woke me with a soft, "Thalia? What's wrong?"

It was Thedar I looked at when I asked, "What do you think Shaarvan would do if I got pregnant?"

"By him or without him?" asked Spelon, laughing at his supposed humor.

I knew not to glare at Spelon like I wanted to. That always turned out badly for me. Instead, I dropped my head and stared down at the log that one of them had placed in front of the building for seating. It seemed like a good place to plop down, so I did.

The males remained silent, waiting for me to explain the question.

I swallowed, took a breath, then sighed. "By Thal," I finally got out. My voice sounded strange, choked up, and whiny. But perhaps this was a suitable time for feeling sorry for myself.

The silence continued. A sudden tenseness invaded Thedar and Tenor's postures. The sour orange of guilt permeated the air, at least from Thedar. Spelon was flowing with gardenias and cherry blossoms, indicating that my dilemma was a source of amusement for him. None of the males reflected any surprise at the news.

"Thal *had* to do it, Thalia. Do you remember our last night on Westla?" Thedar asked.

I nodded "Kind of, but I didn't remember it before, only that Stegthal made us board his ship and leave."

"Having a son will be good for Thal," Spelon said, chuckling as if I'd brought good news. For a moment, I was afraid he'd slap me on the back with his enthusiasm, but he turned and slapped Thedar instead.

I looked around, seeing only smiles and jubilation. They had forgotten me and my part in it.

"You don't understand. It isn't Shaarvan's!" I cried out. I wiggled against the rough texture of the log I was sitting on. The bark had not yet been removed. It was a bit like sitting on a cactus. Did Shapechanger planets have cacti?

"It is your *husband's,* right?" Tenor said, emphasizing what he knew I still didn't accept. He was playing with Thaarac, but his eyes were on my face, and he was lightly probing me.

"Of course, it is the seed of her husband. How dare you insult her!" Spelon's voice bubbled with anger. His fists clenched. The odor of rotten pampa fruit zinged the air.

The Shapechanger all began to argue. Thaarac's thumb plopped into his mouth. His eyes rounded with alarm, but he sat watching them, quiet for once.

"Stop it!" I halted them. Four sets of eyes turned to stare at me. "You don't understand the important question. What will Shaarvan say?"

"Thalia, stop worrying about Shaarvan. If he returns . . ."

"When, Tenor! Not if! When," I reminded him.

"If he returns," Tenor said, ignoring my correction. His eyes held a warning that I should not correct him on the matter again. "Shaarvan will not expect your life to be on freeze."

"Oh, why do I bother? None of you understand!" I stood up, stamped my foot, and glowered at them. "You don't see that my life is in freeze mode. That's exactly what it is, Tenor — a frozen period of waiting that goes on and on. You make it worse because you don't believe that this is all going to end one day. But it will. Shaarvan promised me he'd come for me, and I believe him, even if none of you do. He'll come no matter where I am, no matter how long it's been. But what will he say? How will he feel when he sees that I have a huge belly full of another man's son? That's what I want to know.

11

You're Shapechanger, and you *should* understand, but you don't! You don't understand anything!"

They were all silent. I suppose I should have been surprised they hadn't cut my tirade short using one of their silence commands, but they hadn't. Even Spelon was looking abashed and nonverbal. Perhaps he was thinking up suitable put downs.

My bondmates had all allowed me to yell at them and tell them exactly what I was worrying about. It was kind of them, I guess, but I wasn't thinking that at the moment. I was too busy feeling horrified by the news. Tears were running down my face, and misery was riding my soul. I started to pick up Thaarac, but Thedar waved me on.

"Go cry it out, Thalia," he said. "We shall watch over Thaarac."

I didn't thank him. I just turned and ran, allowing my legs to carry me away from their stunned faces and the sadness in their eyes. I ran to the planet's zebra look-alike. The stubras weren't at all like zebras, though. They were feral animals but gentle as lambs. A stubra was always willing to hear my grief. It would hold perfectly still, head lowered towards me, and bleat softly, soothingly, comforting me each time I desperately needed it. I believe the stubras understood my sorrow the way no one else could.

I had my arms around him and was jabbering away to the little male stubra I'd named Cupid. He was my favorite. He was blabbing sadly, and I was sure he was commiserating with me. I'd only been there a few minutes when I felt Spelon join me. I wished he hadn't.

"I'm all right," I assured him without looking up.

Spelon didn't take my hint and leave. He leaned against the wall and looked like he was planning to stay for a while. He watched me as I hugged and petted Cupid.

"Why do you not find happiness with Thal?" he asked after a moment's silence.

Cupid's coat was wet from my tears. His fur had taken on the odor of a wet dog, yet a stubra had hair nothing like a dog's. The stubra's coats were furry, more as if relations between a cat and a lamb had born fruit.

"I am not unhappy. He is kind to me."

"Does he not meet your needs?"

"My needs?" I said, at first, puzzled until my face heated as I understood Spelon's meaning. I let out a sigh big enough to frighten poor Cupid. The stubra bleated, but he moved in closer, draping his head across my lap.

I heaved another deep breath. "Yes, Spelon. Thal does his duty."

Spelon nodded, crossed his overly muscled arms, and stood leaning again a post in a position that made him look like a statue of Atlas. My gaze never made it to his face. I couldn't bear to see his eyes, which would probably be narrowed by his revulsion at my weaknesses. I'd often wondered if women in Spelon's world were female body builders who bowed down to their males whenever they weren't lifting weights. Or maybe they were robots who reacted to nothing — emotionless and servile androids.

"Then you should be content," Spelon said, summing up his whole concept of womanhood.

As usual, Spelon was not cheering me up; he was making me angry. "Why is it that none of you can understand? I *love* Shaarvan. Can't you appreciate that?"

The arms uncrossed. The Atlas statue shifted. "He is gone, Thalia. Why do you not recognize that fact and accept it?"

How many times must I repeat the same thing over and over? My bondmates were supposed to be Shaarvan's friends, yet they didn't know him at all. Not if they thought he would desert me permanently. Unless they knew something, I didn't. Had he told them he would never come back for me?

I rested my face against the soft, wooly fur of Cupid. The silkiness of its coat reminded me of the feel of Shaarvan's soft pelt of hair. How I wished I could run my hand through it right now, to snuggle into his arms, to kiss his . . .

"Blab, blab?" the stubra asked me.

I patted Cupid's smooth neck and scratched behind his ears.

"Blab," the stubra assured me, his answer to all hardships, all stress.

Spelon continued to stand there, studying me. He understood me the least of all my bondmates, but I knew he cared. Or, at least, I thought he did. I wasn't always sure with him. Like why was he the one who had followed me to my hiding spot? Why hadn't it been Thedar or Tenor? I was closer to them. I sighed, trying to match my sigh to Cupid's blab. Somehow, when I tried to blab, it didn't de-stress me. The heartache remained.

I turned to face Spelon. Speaking calmly, not allowing my voice to rise to the pitch that would accurately match the torment going on inside of me, I said, "I told you. Shaarvan *will* return for me."

Spelon didn't comment. He sat down on the low fence rail that the bondmates had rigged so that the stubras wouldn't poop all over the equipment. The immense Shapechanger looked thoughtful, probably only wondering how many stubras he could lift up at once. Or how much time he had to spend in consoling me . . . Had the other guys sent him, ordered him to pretend to be nice?

I glanced over at him again. "You would tell me if you'd heard something about Shaarvan, wouldn't you?"

Spelon shifted. I could see he was wording his answer carefully to avoid a lie. I watched him even more closely, suddenly alert to the fact that he was hiding something.

"I would tell you what your husband desired you to know," Spelon said.

I bolted up to face him, ready to demand answers. The stubra, frightened by my sudden movement, galumphed off, bleating its complaints to the others. Its fright stopped me from demanding that Spelon tell me whatever it was he knew (a good thing when dealing with a Shapechanger male). I swallowed the words I'd intended to use and studied Spelon's eyes, watching him fidget in a very unShapechanger manner.

"Spit in the wind! You do know something!" I said.

I didn't bother trying to needle Spelon for information. I whirled for the door and ran into the house to query Thal. He was expecting me. I must have projected my discovery all the way from the paddock.

Spelon followed me in. "I told her nothing," he blurted out.

"You did not have to. Thalia is probably Level 7 or 8 by now. Even without probing, she is picking up more."

"How long have you known something?" I demanded angrily, ignoring Thal's analysis.

"Easy, Thalia," he warned.

I breathed in a deep breath, fighting to curb my mouth and the questions writhing in my brain. I knew I would get nothing if I didn't act submissive in my inquiry.

"Thal, please tell me what you've heard."

Thal put down the book he'd been reading, swung his arm around my shoulder, and drew me closer. "All right. I suppose it is time, but there is little we know, and we have heard nothing since we left Westla.

"We suspect that there is a battle for supremacy in Altar. One side is led by Thenos. You can guess the other leader. At least the probability is high."

"Shaarvan is leading an army?" My voice sounded surprised, but hadn't I known it all along? Shaarvan was a leader. He wouldn't be one to follow orders blindly or to stay in the back where he'd be safe. He would always face a problem, drive the action, and put himself foremost into danger. Not to mention the problem of Thenos being his own brother. He must feel guilt for that, although it wasn't his fault.

"I said, the probability is that he's leading the attack. Westla has also sent troops," Thal said, "and I would expect that some of the other Shapechanger-controlled planets have, too. We are all united in ousting Thenos. His crimes are many.

"Hopefully, the added support will be no more than symbolic. Assuming there are commoners who back the non-Thenos-led, there will be no tanks or bombs. That is not our way. Instead, think of cerebral resistance as the Shapechanger attempt to convince Altarians to follow the traditional, government instead of a dictatorship with Thenos.

"If Shaarvan is leading the forces that concentrate on undermining the Power of Thenos, the Shapechanger will use the Mind Force of the Shapechanger. He is very strong, Thalia. I imagine he is good at it. But such battles are engineered by a slow process. How long it will take for victory is the big unknown."

I had moved to face Thal. I slipped my arms around his neck and looked up into his face pleadingly. "Isn't there anything we can do? You say I have Power. And all of you have even more. Couldn't we help? Please?"

Thal's face hardened into tense lines in spite of my soft manner. "We shall do as Shaarvan ordered. We stay here and keep you and Shaarvan's heir safe."

"His son won't even know him," I argued.

"You will keep it that way, Thalia," Thal said, removing my hands from his neck.

Thal's face had solidified into rigidity. The curve of his jaw looked steel-rimmed.

"You forbid me to talk to Thaarac about his father?" I asked, taking a step back.

Behind me, I heard and "felt" Spelon slipping away. Coward!

"Thaarac believes that I am his father," Thal said.

"Then we must remind him of the truth," I said, ignoring my instincts, which were telling me to stop. But it was too big an injustice. Thaarac should be told the truth.

I was determined to win this battle, but I wasn't a complete idiot. I watched Thal carefully for warnings of danger. I knew I treaded in an area that had more landmines than a war zone.

But Thal's eyes did not flare as I expected. They were merely thoughtful as he answered me. "Even if the truth endangers Thaarac's life?"

I gasped, then probed him, trying to pull out the information. Unable to do so, I shook my head. "There is no one on this planet. You said so. How can it be dangerous for Thaarac to know the truth?"

"We do not know what Thenos will do next, but is it worth the chance? We have no knowledge of where we will be forced to flee if we leave here. Maybe we will be lucky enough to stay until Altar's troubles end, but there is always the possibility that we cannot. Soon, Thaarac will be talking more. Then, the danger increases."

I could tell that Thal meant well, and one order from him would have silenced me anyway. I didn't understand why it was so bad for Thaarac to know who his father was, but I'd pushed as hard as I dared. I bowed to Thal's wisdom and let the matter drop.

Thal read my thought, took my hand, and lifted it to his mouth to kiss it. I knew that I had pleased him.

There were other issues swirling around in my mind. "Thal, I don't understand any of this. Thenos is not much older than I am. How could he have risen to a place in the government so high that it would lead to this kind of conflict, of war?

The tension I'd felt in Thal eased. He picked up a curl of my hair and toyed with it. His eyes once again softened as he looked at me. I felt like purring.

"Come. We will sit down so I can explain. I think it is time you understand what's happening on Altar," he said with a calmness that belied the fact that I'd been digging for information all this time.

Our seating arrangements left much to be desired. A roughhewn wood framework formed the base. Inside the sitting portion, the males and I had fitted reeds across the couch to soften the seat, but the weedy plants we'd used were scratchy when they dried out. They didn't seem to break apart, making them semi-permanent padding, but they pierced through the fabric of my dress — much more than they did with the males' pants, which were thicker and sturdier than the Terran jean material I used to wear. Thal had told me that we would cover the sofa with furs, but the only animals we'd come across so far were the stubras, and none of us wanted to kill them.

Thedar had told us that there must be predators somewhere, or the stubras would have overrun the planet, but that didn't seem to be true. So far, we'd seen no young stubras. Perhaps the attrition was due to their lack of baby-making.

How easily an itchy seat made one's mind wander. I corralled it and prodded Thal.

"How do you know? Have you been in contact with them? I thought we couldn't . . ."

"No, Thalia. None of us has spoken to anyone since the day we left Westla. All I know is what Tem told me before we left."

I was wiggling with distress by then. The reeds were like mosquitoes, biting only certain people, or at least it felt like that.

"Stand up," Thal said. He grabbed a blanket he'd been using earlier for Thaarac, covered the couch, and waved for me to sit back down.

"Better?" he asked.

When I nodded, he continued. "I think I have a fair picture of Thenos' rise to power. Thenos visited Westla for a time. He and

19

Shaarvan needed testing. It was determined then that Thenos had all the charisma and the Power of Shaarvan, but the tests revealed that he had none of Shaarvan's morals. Due to that, Thenos failed his leadership tests."

Despite the blanket, the reeds were still poking at my lower extremities. I was trying not to wiggle, but Thal must have taken note. He tugged me into his lap, form-fitted me for his comfort, and then pulled me back against his back.

I no longer fought such things. I had accepted his right to my governance (most of the time.) As his arms encircled me, I said nothing, just waited for him to continue.

He kissed my cheek and continued. "Shaarvan, in case you didn't know, excelled at the Westlan tests. He was rated as high as Tem, which is why he will one day be Westla's leader. Shaarvan presently stands as Second of Westla, although he has never made the commitment to leave Altar. Shaarvan seems to prefer one foot in each realm."

I hadn't really understood all that before. It was something else the Shapechanger had kept from me. I suppose that was understandable while I was brain-wiped from my slave days on Freinana, but Shaarvan could have told me after I Shapechanged — when I got my memories back. But after that, he'd been distanced, too caught up in discussions with the Shapechanger on Westla, too busy with arranging for my guardians and Second husband. Or maybe it had just been like it always was — I didn't need to know because I was owned by my Shapechanger husband and must merely obey his wishes.

Thal had grown silent, probably riding my thoughts. He could do that without a focused scan. But if he was reading me, he didn't say anything. He just waited for me to redirect my thoughts back to Thenos.

"Is there more?" I asked, weaving my arm through his and leaning in to rest my head against his comfortably large shoulder.

Thal chuckled softly and patted my hand. He kissed my cheek and nuzzled my neck, sending amazingly warm sensations throughout my body.

The truth was that no matter how busy Thal was, it seemed that my initiation of any kind of body touching was appreciated. I guess I didn't do it often enough. I'd rebelled for so long, fought him so hard, and now . . . Everything was different. My guardians were right. Thal really was my husband, and I needed him for more than just friendship. He was the father of my — our child and the lover of my nights. He was what Shaarvan used to be — my comfort, my confidant, and the pillar I leaned on.

"Always," he responded, sliding right into my reflections.

I sighed, then nodded and closed my eyes, breathing in his scent. Sometimes, Thal smelled of eucalyptus. Other times, like old books or the chemicals he'd been working with. It was never an always thing. Yet, I knew the smell of him. I could have passed the First Test, identifying him from surrounding Shapechanger. It wasn't necessary to capture a whiff of his individual Shapechanger odor. It was the sense of him, the knowing, as sure as sight or the tone of his voice.

"Yes," he said. "We are bonded, my dear. That is what you feel."

Maybe. Yet, I knew his touch and his mind contact, at least when he meant me to.

Thal cleared his throat. "Shall I peel the rest of the bark off?"

What? But before the question sprang from my lips, I understood the meaning of it. "Please."

He issued another pat on the hand, a quick squeeze as he enfolded my hand, and then he continued. "The testing, as I said, revoked all Thenos' rights in the line of leadership, but apparently that did not stop Thenos' ambition. He used his time on Westla for other purposes. Somehow, he discovered things from the Old Ones that had been kept secret for hundreds of Passes. Tem thinks that Thenos may have unearthed a potion that took away the power of a Shapechanger lord, a potion that took not only his Power but his vitality.

That is a supposition, but Tem has proof about the second potion Thenos stole. It was an artificial booster. It made Thenos even more Powerful, and it hid his thoughts from others. After he began taking the drug, neither the Old Ones on Westla nor the Elders on Altar could read the evil taking over his soul. That is why no one was alarmed by the earlier stages of Thenos' cruelty — they were all drug-blinded to it.

"When Thenos first met you on Altar, he had just returned from a second trip to Westla. Tem believes that Thenos must have smuggled out more of the drugs at that time. An old Shapechanger, Baltoff by name, was caught manufacturing the Power enhancing drug. Baltoff was banned from Westla. I think he went to live on Clofa, one of Altar's two moons. At his trial, Baltoff gave a great deal of information about Thenos' plans. It was Baltoff who gave us the history I have just relayed to you.

"Are you okay hearing about this, my sweet wife?"

I nodded. I needed Thal to continue. I needed to know.

"Thenos was banned from Westla. He can never go back there. But the damage was already done, we know now. He had the potions in his body and in the hold of his father's ship, and when he returned to Altar, it is assumed that he used the first drug on the Elders.

"Shaarvan's father discovered Thenos digging deeply into the foundations of Altar's government. He tried to stop him, but Thenos had established himself too well by that point. Tem thinks that Thenos used various criminals to do his nefarious deeds. It seems there are always those who are willing to serve one more reprehensible than they are. One of them kidnapped you and injected Shaarvan with the drug that almost killed him.

I inhaled sharply. My pain was still raw from the memories of the slaver who sold me and the commoner who bought me. The latter, Isandor, had raped and beaten me for a halfPass.

"I know, my darling. Both of them both paid for their crimes, but the wounds inside you are deep. I respect that, and I admire you for surviving. I am so very glad that you held on."

I blinked back my tears and urged Thal to tell me the rest that he knew.

"The Elders of Altar, except for Shaarvan's father, all mysteriously died within days of each other. Shaarvan is sure that Thenos is to blame for that, a logical conclusion based on what we learned from Baltoff. Tevor, Shaarvan's father, and yours, of course, has lapsed into a coma. He may no longer be alive."

"No," I cried out. "Tevor was kind. He was a good Shapechanger. Poor Teea."

"The Elders of Altar were all gone or disabled in Tevor's case. Thenos dissolved the government and forbid the formation of a new Council. Thus, a government fell, and a tyrant rose. Now there is war in Altar between the Commoners with Thenos in command and the Shapechanger."

"With Shaarvan in command," I said, sighing heavily.

"Probably," Thal said.

"Is there anything else?"

"Not since the day we left, my dear. Now you know what we know. Was it worth it? Is it too great a burden for your delicate shoulders?"

"No. Thank you, Thal. I appreciate being told,"

"It was time."

He was staring out through what I called the melted candy window. I wondered what his thoughts were. I didn't have to ponder. He began speaking, not to me, but to himself.

"Thenos is insane due to the drugs, but he is also Powerful. And only Shaarvan stands in his way. It has always been so. Shaarvan and Thenos are two strong forces, and the rest are like moons orbiting large planets. Shaarvan attracts his field of moons and Thenos, another grouping. Of course, in astronomy, forces of greater gravity do not bomb little children."

Thal was not making sense. I knew he'd forgotten I was there. He did that at times. His voice changed, and he used astronomy analogies. I was usually careful to stay quiet, but this time, with his mind wide open, his thoughts made me shiver.

"What do you mean, bomb little children?" I asked.

Thal stared at me, but he still didn't see me. His eyes were focused on Tessa's telling him about the explosion at Shaarvan's nursery. He was picturing the site — the bodies of children, limbs twisted, faces with unseeing eyes.

"Spit on Barquel!" I said in shock and bolted up and away from Thal.

"Thalia!" Thal was back to me again. I felt his mind slam shut. My head throbbed from his ejection, but the pain didn't dull my horror.

"You never told me," I said, shaking so hard my teeth rattled in my mouth. Thaarac could have been killed if . . . all those poor children! How horrible!"

I had a fuzzy memory of Tessa telling us. I had been there when she recounted it. Why hadn't I remembered?

Thal took me into his arms. "Thalia, forgive me. I did not intend for you to know. It is a sadness I would not have you carry."

I trembled from the dreadfulness of such a thing, but anger at being kept from knowing flooded me as well. "You need to stop sheltering me. Tell me the truth. You kept me ignorant, and then you called me a child because I argued over leaving Westla."

Thal's hands pulled me against his chest. In his arms, my shaking calmed. His hand stroked my head. "Women are not made to carry heavy burdens, Thalia."

I pushed away. He allowed it, but his hands on my arms kept me from backing further.

"I was stolen from my planet and made to adapt to a new language and to aliens. I was a slave to a man who raped me and beat me. I was given in marriage to a Second husband. How can you think I am fragile?"

Thal's eyes smiled, amused but not impressed. "You have always had a male to take care of you, and you always will, Thalia. Fragile or not, there is no need for you to be weighed down by distress. That is a male's responsibility."

I wanted to argue with him and rail against his ridiculous beliefs, but he already knew my thoughts. He was watching my eyes, still reading me. I looked down, wishing I could shut him out as he had done with me.

On Westla, I'd almost lost my son, and yet I'd still argued for what I wanted, not for what was. Why hadn't I heard the truth, the way it was, the danger? Perhaps I hadn't acted like a child but more like a stubborn-minded fool.

"Thal," I said, looking up into his eyes, "Would you hold me, please?"

"Gladly, my wife," he responded, and I knew my request gave him pleasure. And there *was* comfort in the strong arms that held me close.

Tren

The Chants, the Legends, I had sung the Shapechanger songs so many times I felt like roaring. Would the Old Ones never stop demanding it of me? Would they never cease their endless litany of "Tell us one more time"?

Why were the Old Ones involved in training me anyway? I had spoken to some of the Shapechanger, and they had told me they had never heard of the Old Ones instructing a neophyte. Why were they interested in me? Why did the Old Ones never answer questions I asked? Why did they always drag out another tale, another legend, and make me learn it? Couldn't their answers be straightforward for once? When would I be done with all their indoctrination?

My questions reminded me again of Shaara. Where was she with her thousand questions? Was Shaarvan treating her well? Did she love him now? Had she remembered her life before?

"Tell us about the Somber Tree," one of the most cantankerous of the Oldsters asked.

"No," I said. "I won't say . . ."

"You will not leave until your grammar is precise. We have told you that a male does not use the shortened form."

"And it is 'shall' with 'I' and 'we,' " Telldan repeated. His cat whiskers rarely lost their shadow now. I saw the soft black and yellow mottling of a partial Change.

"Are you saying there is an end to this?" I asked. I addressed my question to Salpar, who always seemed to be the most inclined to respond.

"Indeed," he said. "The end is your completion."

There were many levels to the meaning of that word. For the rest of the day, I brooded over it, swatting it about with both paws.

Thalia

It was strange being pregnant. I seemed to crave Thal more and more. Tessa had told him that the only way to keep me from the Snow was to plant his seed in me, but was it possible that my holding his son in my womb bound us more tightly as well?

I no longer cried when our joining was over, and I cherished the moments of closeness that followed. Thal would hold me in his strong, warm arms, and sometimes he, like Shaarvan, would recite poetry. His poems were about the stars, the planets, and the heavens. Often, I fell asleep with his words in my mind. I think it was because of those poems that I began to dream about them. One vision I had night after night. In it, I was riding a comet to Pluto.

I'd long ago asked Thal if he knew of Earth. He'd studied our planet and understood more than I of Earth's Solar System. Many nights, we talked of it.

Yet, the dream I kept having disturbed me. Why would I ride a comet when we had a perfectly good spaceship? Why would I go to Pluto when my home was Earth? The dream repeated over and over. Finally, I told Thal about it.

"Interesting," he said, but he looked at me strangely and changed the conversation.

He did not volunteer the information that there was a Pluto on Altar. I read it in his mind one night. It was the ice cap of Altar, the polar region. Was I trying to find a way to Shaarvan, with a bulging belly, and on the back of a comet? That was laughable.

Yet, from then on, Thal asked me to tell him every dream I had. I tried, but I couldn't always remember them. Often, they took place in icy gopher-like burrows that men walked in. One night, I dreamed of Shaarvan. He was layered in jackets, but his skin was furred in a half-change. He was looking up at Clofa, Altar's first moon. I was seeing the moon through his eyes when there was a giant red flare. It burst out into the blackness, like an erupting volcano. Shaarvan cried out, and men came running to stare up at Clofa. I heard their words. A moon colony had been destroyed. The men and the Shapechanger wept. Their tears froze on their faces. One of them led Shaarvan back inside.

The dream was so real I woke up crying. Thal's arms cradled me until I stopped sobbing. Then we talked. Later, he rode me until the dream no longer held my thoughts. In the morning, I scarcely remembered it, but Thal looked at me peculiarly and seemed preoccupied throughout the day.

It was funny, too, that about that time, I always felt cold. I supposed it was due to my advancing pregnancy. I wore jackets when the Shapechanger remained bare-chested.

"Why do you look at me like that?" I asked them.

"For one thing, because it is a hot day, and you shiver in your coat," Spelon replied.

I was never warm, and my dreams each night were of snow, ice, and frozen tunnels with drifts packed higher than a Shapechanger's body.

"It's the babe on the way that takes your heat," Thal said.

My bondmates agreed, but they watched me, and I felt their uneasiness.

One night, bundled in blankets thick as Thal's arm, I dreamed of an ocean, frozen so solid that men walked on it, pulling heavy sleds. I saw Shaarvan again, breathing out great clouds of smoke into the frozen air.

A woman laid her head on his shoulder. I started to cry out with the agony of his betrayal, but I saw that it was Teea, his mother. Where was Tevor?

Then my vision moved on, and I saw Pathe with a young Shapechanger girl. He was treating her wound, but there was a deep affection for her in his eyes. Who was she? Where was Goria?

I didn't want to tell my dream to Thal. "It is not fair that you comfort me and care for me, and I dream only of Shaarvan and Altar," I said after I'd relayed it.

"Perhaps you work it out of your system that way," Thal responded, but his mind was closed to me.

I hoped Thal was right. But a more urgent worry was what I'd do if I saw Shaarvan with a female in his arms, one who wasn't Teea.

One night, buried down between a bundle of blankets, I woke up from a nightmare, screaming.

"What is it, Thalia? Tell me. Was it Shaarvan?"

"He came here, and he saw me. He was angry with me. He kept asking me where Shaarac was. I told him there was no more Shaarac, but he didn't seem to care. Then he demanded to know if the babe in my stomach was his. Why would he ask me that, Thal? He would know it was not. He ordered me to tell him the name of the planet where we were hiding."

I was shaking from the horror of it. It was a nightmare, wasn't it? Just my mind (or my guilt, a la Freud) playing tricks. But it had seemed so real, and my body had felt repulsed by Shaarvan — if it was Shaarvan, which I somehow doubted.

"Thal, it wasn't like my other dreams. It felt different."

"Did you give him the name of this planet? Think, Thalia. It is important to remember."

I shook my head. "No. The things he said made no sense. If Shaarvan were here, I mean, if a dream could really bring him here, why would he ask me where the planet was? He would know."

I was sitting up, rubbing my eyes, although I was no longer sleepy. I felt nauseated, and I craved a bath. My skin practically writhed in distaste.

And then I knew. Shaarvan would never have repelled me. But Thenos could change his age and his appearance. It was Thenos who had crept into my dreams. But how? Why?

I told Thal what I'd just realized, but he didn't seem surprised.

"It's strange, Thal. I used to think Thenos and Shaarvan were similar, but Thenos only wanted me to think so. He isn't at all like Shaarvan. Thenos is mean. He's filled with greed and hate. I find him as repulsive as Isandor used to be."

"Yes, I know, my sweet. Go back to sleep now, my love," Thal said. "Thenos cannot hurt you, not this far away."

When I woke up in the morning, the males were preparing for our departure. All our beautiful constructions stayed on Deadstar. My garden, which was bearing vegetables, just like Thal had promised, without us, would die. No one would be there to water it. I cried, but I didn't argue. If Thal said we needed to leave, I knew to trust him.

Thenos

I did it! I made contact with my princess again. I entered her lovely mind. I could feel the sweet essence of her and almost touch the warmth of her body. Stars, she makes me long for her. My organ grew heavy and full. It has not functioned so with any other female for a long time. Yet, with my princess, I know it will hold its engorgement until I am satiated. With her in my bed, I shall regain my vigor and my lusting thrust. I must have her. Even if I have to leave Altar and grab her myself, I shall have her.

It pleases me that my princess is far more Powerful than ever. She calls out, even from a great distance. I do not know where they have taken her, but she is no longer on Westla. Who has her under his Power? Whose bed does she sleep in? Curse Shaarvan for Seconding her to another. No other male deserves her obedience and her body in his bed. I shall kill the Warlord who Seconded her. His agony will last for Tides.

My princess has another spawn in her belly. That displeases me to the highest degree. I should have been the one to plant that seed. It is only I who is worthy of her. I shall have it killed . . . unless . . .

Who knows of this babe? Perhaps I should allow her to bear it. Then, I could proclaim it mine, and there would be no outstretched belly and a halfPass of interrupted pleasure. Which Warlord has Shaarvan tied her to? Is he high enough to produce a worthy heir? Why should I waste such a perfect opportunity?

I shall seize my princess, and the boy will be mine. Besides, the baby will comfort her when little Shaarac dies from some tragic accident. I do not long to see the tears of my little princess. I shall attempt to provide for her happiness with a few trifling kindnesses. After all, she will be the queen of Altar, but she is still only a woman.

Ah, but what a woman! My sword is still hard. Perhaps I shall visit one of my play toys. No sense in letting such a bonus go to waste . . .

Shaara

For a while, on the ship, the dreams of Shaarvan stopped. I missed them dreadfully. We journeyed on the ship for a quarterTide before they returned. I dreamed that Teea was talking to Shaarvan. I wondered why they couldn't see me. I tried so hard to catch their attention. I thought Shaarvan noticed me spying on their conversation, but he turned away.

"I know she is happy now, but the ache of missing her is strong," Shaarvan was saying to his mother. "It seems almost as if she were here at times. Like now, I feel I could reach out my hand and touch her fingers," my beloved said.

"Do, Shaarvan, please do it," I begged him, but the dream faded. I cried, my fingers raised in the air, empty of his touch.

Thal woke. "Shaarvan again? In the ice?"

I nodded.

"Come, my dear. I shall hold you until you sleep."

The dreams were with me almost every night from then on: snippets of scenery, a conversation, or a glance at Shaarvan's face through Teea's eyes.

Once, I heard Teea speak. "I, too, feel Shaara, too, at times. She shares my eyes when I look at you. I hope it is a true sending. I would like to give her that comfort."

One night, Shaarvan was not at Pluto but in a bubblecar. He was far from the ice and snow, traveling over rocks and sand. *"Where are you going?"* I asked him softly.

"I must be going crazy. I hear your soft, lovely voice, Shaara, even in my waking hours."

"I love you for always and always."

"I wish I could tell you how much I love you. Woman-talk or not, I would tell you I love you if I could, Shaara, my soulmate."

I was still saying, *"I love you always and always,"* over and over when Thal woke me.

"I hear your words Thalia, but I doubt they are for me. Rest, my love, rest."

He looked so sad. I kissed his eyebrow and his lips and fell into a deep, quiet sleep.

It was a twentyTide before our ship finally reached its destination. Thal would tell none of us where we were. I knew it was me he mistrusted, but I didn't care where we were as long as the nights were Shaarvan's.

Our destination this time turned out not to be a planet but a moon. I had thought such satellites were barren and rocky, but this one was beautiful. It was filled with plant life and water, and the air smelled sweet. I'd never have realized it was a moon except that its sky was filled with a big planet that loomed down at us with a brown, craggy face. As we revolved around it, the browns turned chocolate and dark, like coffee grounds. I was glad Thal had chosen the moon as our new home.

When we landed and I was allowed to walk down the ramp, I was as cheerful as I'd ever been since Shaarvan left. The grass beneath us quivered in the wind. The smell of flowers and trees tickled my nose, and the morning dew filled me with delight. It was wonderful to be on land again.

Our arrival was a mirror of our landing on Deadstar. All progressed in the same fashion — the camouflaging of the ship, the building of the houses, the waterway, and the garden . . . only the wild stubras were gone. Thankfully, Thal had cargoed the four we'd trained, which was a very good thing because this moon had no animals that were docile enough to use for work.

Unfortunately, there were several species of large predators. My freedom to walk about was withdrawn. Spelon made me promise I wouldn't even step outside the house without a guard.

I offered right away to learn how to shoot a pipe weapon, but the males acted like I'd suggested something horrendous. I was told again how it was forbidden for a woman to touch a weapon. (What were they afraid of, that I'd turn into a malicious executioner or that the weapon might melt at my touch?)

I only argued a little bit, but Spelon killed one of the predators and brought it to me to see. At first, I laughed when I saw it. It was small and looked like it would be no threat. But then Spelon nudged its mouth open, and I saw the double row of sharp teeth. It could have ripped a metal pole into two pieces with one bite. My Second explained that the animal hunted the large bovine animals of the forests and woods. The predator was not only fierce but would charge anything that moved.

"It attacks the herbivores' feet, severing the sinews of their muscles so that the much larger animal cannot escape," Spelon added. "If it caught you wandering in the woods, Thalia, it would find no difficulty in bringing you down. One bite, and your ankles . . ."

"Please stop, Spelon," I cried out, vexed by his harping on it. "I get it."

"She is right," Tenor defended me. "You have made your point. Thalia is too intelligent to stray from the clearing here."

"Even the clearing is dangerous for her. She must never be left unattended," Spelon argued. "Nor the other child."

"Other child?" I huffed, hurt by his daily dose of put down.

Only Tharaac's attack on Spelon's legs saved me from more lectures (or from arguing with Spelon about his nastiness.)

Thal had brought the toddler outside for a needed break. Spelon picked up the little one and swung him atop his huge muscled shoulders, draping legs around a neck so thick, the predator probably couldn't have bitten through it. (Admittedly, a tiny bit of exaggeration, but I was peeved.) Thaarac, not catching on to his mother's annoyance with the big guy, squealed with joy.

Thal stayed with us for a while. He was fascinated with the predator that Spelon had killed. My husband examined its teeth and, upon hearing Spelon deliver the same lecture on the animal's hunting practices, seconded Spelon's orders for me to remain inside my prison.

It was Thal's suggestion that we use the carcass for our protection. He and the others butchered the creature and scented our house with its odor. I hated the smell, but Thal was right — we were no longer bothered by bovine invasions of our garden after that, and the predator's skin did make an excellent scarecrow. It flapped in the winds like a weather vane and warned us of approaching storms.

Days later, I saw that each male was wearing the predator's teeth around their neck. Spelon told me that the teeth could cut through anything, including the tough fibers of the Belloparb tree, which produced rope and material for writing, as well as the utensils we used at meals, but I wondered if the necklaces were a sign the males were retreating to their caveman days. Weren't teeth necklaces a way to display bravery and skill?

Because of the predator, Tenor called a *Bozune,* both Thaarac and I spent a great deal of our time inside the house. I hated that. Thal did allow me to take a walk with Spelon each afternoon, but we never went far. Sometimes, I took Thaarac with me, but Thal, more often than not, would tell me I needed a break. Then, Thal would push back his work and spend time with Thaarac.

Sometimes, Tenor or Thedar would go with us. We would journey all the way into the woods then, but those walks were never long enough. A snarl in the bushes or the scent of the *Bozune* would make the Shapechanger return me to the house immediately.

Thal guarded me whenever I labored in the garden, but he was becoming increasingly uneasy with my working there, not because of the predator but because of my advancing pregnancy. One day, Thal handed the garden over to Tenor, and that was that. I was no longer allowed to pull weeds or channel the water. I loved my garden and the stalky green vegetables that grew so quickly, but a flashed "no argument" signal ended any discussion.

Thal's over-protectiveness was ridiculous. My belly had begun to bulge more and more, but it didn't hamper me. I ran, skipped, and giggled at everything. I loved this new world we were on. The air was sweet. The clouds were almost always puffy and white, and even in the rain, which poured down on us at least once a day, this moon that was now our abode seemed magical.

I wasn't all that frightened by the *Bozune*. I could still change my shape. No matter how fierce the predator, I didn't think it would fight me in my Saberey form. I supposed I could even change into a *Bozune*, theoretically. Would my scent be the same? Would a *Bozune* accept me as one of them?

Spelon and Thal wouldn't discuss such an idea, but Tenor said it was an interesting thought. Had I considered that all the predators they'd killed so far had been male? How did the animal treat its females? Was I ready to test it out? Tenor asked.

Since a Shapechanger cannot change gender, I decided that, until we knew more about the species, Tenor was probably right that I shouldn't Shapechange.

Despite the cocooning that the predator forced on me, I was as content as one of our blabbing stubra and too wrapped up in my happiness to notice that all was not well with Thal.

One day, we were heading for the brook that supplied us with our water. It was my favorite destination, not only because it was a pleasant, relaxing place to sit but because I often got to see some of the native wildlife that wandered over to drink unless Tharaac got too chatty and scared them away.

"Are you and Thal fighting?" Spelon suddenly asked. I shot a look behind us at Tenor carrying my son and further behind him at Thedar with his pipe gun in readiness.

"No, of course not. I would be black and blue," I said, laughing. I bent over to pick up a pretty yellow flower. It was not easy to do that anymore. Reaching down had a major obstacle in the way.

"Stop it, Thalia. I shall pick them for you," Spelon said.

I watched Spelon fondly as he rushed forward to grab a handful. His giant hands were more used to fighting than picking wild flowers. He crushed most of the wild blooms, but I thanked him anyway as he handed them to me.

Spelon urged me to sit. Although I was not tired, I could see he had something to discuss with me.

"Thal does not look well," Spelon said.

"He is Shapechanger. Of course, he's fine."

"No, Thalia. I do not believe so."

I teased Spelon with a flower, running it along his neck. "Oh, Spelon, you are turning into a worrywart!" I said, giggling. I urged Spelon to speak of other things, but after a while, I looked hard and long at Thal. Spelon was right. Thal didn't look healthy anymore.

Later, back at our house, I questioned my husband. He had been writing in his journal, as always, keeping his meticulous notes on the sky. He paused and looked up at me. Then he smiled, but I saw that the smile didn't reach the sadness in his eyes. I touched his arm, wanting an answer. Again, the corners of his mouth tilted upward for a moment. He put down his book and patted the seat next to him (a new couch made entirely from the trunk and tough fibers of the Belloparb tree, which didn't scratch as much as the reed couch before it.) I sat beside Thal and put my hand on his leg.

He patted me and covered my hand with his. "Thalia, you must not worry. I am simply feeling my age," he said in a scratchy, gruff voice. He stretched out his legs and crossed them at the ankles. His feet were bare. I liked the look of Thal's feet, long and narrow, his big toe twice the size of the others.

"I am an old man in this young body," he said. His left hand reached up to cup my chin. He turned my face to meet his. "That should be enough to make me content, but it is not."

I started to question him, but his finger touched my mouth, the signal for silence.

He smiled. "Shaarvan is a lucky Shapechanger, my dear."

I understood the problem then. Thal was jealous of my nightly dreams of Shaarvan. But what could I say? The silence command was on me. And what would I have said, even if he'd allowed me to speak? I couldn't stop the dreams, nor could I stop loving Shaarvan. Ever.

I hugged Thal, kissed him on the mouth, and then led him to our bed. I tried my hardest to do patterns on him. He laughed at that and wove his own spells. For a time, all was good between us.

Tren

Tessa finally told me that Shaara was not on Westla. All that time, I had walked through the corridors, searching faces, examining faraway women, hoping that I would see her. I used to sit at the Bisbawn Cafe, where strollers passed on their way to the mountains and the forests. I was sure she would appear one day. I was prepared with the words I would use and the manner of my approach. But Shaara never appeared, and my disappointment soured many hours.

Why had the Old Ones never told me? Why had they ignored my constant questions concerning Shaara? Did they believe I would cause trouble with Shaarvan? Did they think that I would attempt to steal her from her husband?

I would not. But I would have rested more contentedly had I known she had regained her memories, that she now loved her husband, and that she was happy. If they distrusted me so, why did they bring me here? Why did they make me a Shapechanger if they feared I would try to steal Shaara from Shaarvan? None of it made sense.

Surely, Shaarvan hadn't believed I would interfere. Hadn't he left me that day with his pledge of friendship? Hadn't I made it clear to him I accepted that Shaara was his?

I pondered it for several days. I knew I could get no more information from Tessa. She babbled about things I did not understand. Her incoherence confused me. Yet the Old Ones heeded her words. I suppose they found meaning where I did not.

Tessa told the Old Ones that I needed to leave. She said it was necessary for me to go find Shaara. But if Shaarvan had wanted that, wouldn't he have told me so himself? He could have stopped by my hospital bed and asked me to go with them or asked me to join them later.

When I said that to Tessa, she always chanted, "You entwined her. You can find her."

Entwined Shaara in what? And how was I supposed to find her when none of them knew where she had gone? I felt like I was living in a madhouse.

41

At Tessa's insistence, they gave me a ship. The Old Ones said it was a present because I didn't ask to become a Shapechanger and was forced to do so. I should have been delighted. But I was hesitant. Would Shaarvan want me to intrude? Would he welcome my presence wherever they were? Besides, I didn't need their guilt gift. I could have bought any ship I desired five times over. But in the end, I accepted it.

That day, when I set out for the trip to the Space Port to claim my new ship, Tem, the head of Westla, and all the Old Ones I had worked with walked me there. They stood about in a farewell ceremony, bowing to me as if I were some great personage, although I was surely the lowest of the lows, having only just become Shapechanger. Tessa stood beside them. The High Priestess never bowed, of course, but she'd come to see me off. She even walked halfway up the ship's ramp with me, stopping to give me her mysterious advice before retreating back down to the others.

"Find Shaara," Tessa had ordered me, cackling like a food bird. "She will need you, but not as much as your new Altarian brother. Shaarvan's need will be much, much greater. A Priestess can go inward to gather strength. Shaarvan is still stuck in old rhymes and beliefs. Your task will be to help him *see* new routes."

Okay. That certainly didn't add much meaning to my undertaking. Of course, when I asked for details, Tessa turned and walked away. Why was I not surprised?

The ship was small, a three person at the most. It wasn't Altarian or Westlan, but instead, some other planet's manufacture. Perhaps the Old Ones just wanted to get rid of it. But, it was a good ship. When I tested it for problems, everything worked well. The supplies were full, and the rooms were set up adequately. It was not luxurious, at least by my standards, but I couldn't expect a traveling casino.

After I'd figured out the system, become used to the technology available, and located the rooms for eating, sleeping, and exercising, I sat down in the pilot's chair and thought the whole thing over. It was craziness — no flight plan, no destination, no idea where Shaara could be. But as I'd thought, the Old Ones and Tessa were all mad. I guess I could play that game. At least I was getting off Westla.

Yet, as I lifted up through the Saberey eye and let my mind be the direction of my flight, I felt nothing. They were wrong. I couldn't feel Shaara or my brother, Shaarvan. There was no mysterious pull as Tessa had promised me.

I set the ship on hover, ate a meal, worked out on the mats, shapeshifted back and forth a couple of times for practice, then decided to head to my bunk.

I'll admit that as I lay on the bed, I wondered if the Old Ones and Tessa had just gotten tired of my questions and released me to relieve their stress. As glad as I was to be free of them, I felt as if they'd rejected me. Had they truthfully decided to flush me out of Westla and send me on a purposeless errand?

And even more strange than that, I'd thought they wanted me to stay away from Shaara, yet now they said they were sending me to her. And why was it that every time I'd asked about Shaarvan, the Old Ones only spoke of Shaara? Shaarvan was my new brother. She was forbidden. Unless something had happened to Shaarvan? Was I a replacement? Why did Shaara need me? Who was watching over her?

Sleep didn't come easily. Perhaps my sleep cycle was too disrupted by my worries and the many, many questions that the Old Ones and Tessa refused to answer. But at last, I slipped into oblivion, only to ride the dreams that Tessa had talked of. When I woke, I took the ship out of hover and set off on the course that I knew with certainty would bring me to Shaara's side. As the ship flew through space, I worked out harder than I'd done before. I kept thinking that I might be going into combat. If I must battle someone to protect my Freinanan waif, so be it. I'd be ready.

Thalia

Thaarac already prefers to be with the males. He has taken Spelon as his favorite, but all of them draw his interest more than his fat, slow-moving mother. Even in the house, his chunky little legs move him forever towards Thal. And Thal, always busy poring over his books, stops and talks with the tot and puts him on his knee for wild rides.

Thaarac likes to feed the animals, though, and he still does that with me. His stocky little hands toss the grain all about him, and then he asks for more. Sometimes, he feeds the stubras from his bare hand and giggles when their whiskers tickle. Often, I let him ride little Partha or Cupid. Thaarac's fat, little legs cling on tightly, and his laugh no longer scares them. They toss their heads and prance slightly, proud to be his steed.

I tell Thaarac at those times about the landoors, but I do not think he believes me. He thinks that landoors could not really be bigger than our little stubras. He laughs when I tell him how I soared over obstacles while on Crimson's back. Thaarac's eyes fall to my stomach, and he smiles and says, "Mommy fat. Mommy no ride."

The others laugh to hear him say that. I think Tenor spurs him on. He thinks it's funny because a Shapechanger is never fat. But I look down and wonder if I will ever be thin again. Sometimes, it's hard for me to remember how I once was free to run. Landoors, even for me, seem like a faraway dream, and I wonder if Thaarac is right to laugh. I miss my independence and the freedom of those days.

Now, when I attempt to do anything, even lifting Thaarac onto Partha's or Cupid's back, there is always a Shapechanger scolding me. And then my son is stolen away, and I am ordered to sit down and rest. I have long ago stopped arguing with males. So I comply until the bondmate is out of sight, and then I do as I wish. I cannot bear to sit long. I am too restless.

Thandar, as Thal has named the son I carry, has taken up kicking my insides as his exercise. It delights me to feel the life within me. Thandar does not kick as hard as Thaarac did, but he is more active. I talk to him a great deal about life and how I look forward to his birth. Thal also has begun to tell him stories in the evening. It is a good time, this period of expectation.

In the night, Thandar distracts me from my dreams, but I cannot blame him for it. It is only when he sleeps that I can journey to my love.

One night in my dreams, I saw Shaarvan leading a troop of men. They were practicing a military maneuver with pipe weapons. I did not dare interrupt, but Shaarvan dodged into a tent and cried out to me, "*Shaara, my love, my soul. It is you. Are you well?*"

"*Yes, but I miss you so. It is an ache of emptiness where my heart used to beat.*"

"*Much better than twinkle, twinkle, little star, my poet wife.*"

"*I am Shapechanger now,*" I teased him.

"*I love you.*"

"*Oh, Shaarvan. I am yours forever.*"

It was too short a contact, but I could not help being ecstatic. We had done it! Across planets and stars, we had forged a link. I fell asleep with a smile on my face, buoyed with the knowledge that Shaarvan still loved me.

I couldn't wait to go to bed after that so I could dream of Shaarvan, but for two days and nights, there was nothing — no dreams, no visions. I paced the floor until Thal commanded me to lie down.

"Thandar disturbs you?" Thal asked.

"No, I am just jittery," I said, but he knew. I could not hide anything from Thal. He immediately made me negate my lie before it made me sick.

"There is a solar flare in Begdar. The red star could be interfering with your dreams," Thal said, and he put his arm around me and pulled me close.

"I wish it would stop."

"Close your eyes, my little one. Perhaps that will bring the dreams."

I snuggled up against him and fell asleep.

A few days later, Shaarvan was on a lookout post, surveying the area.

"Shaarvan, can you talk?" I asked.

"I am alone, my love. Do you have a question? I can always tell."

"Did you tell Thal he could join with me?"

"Yes, Shaara. Of course, it was required."

"But . . ."

"You would argue across the stars?"

"Shaarvan, how could you?"

"Because I had to, my love. You are Shapechanger."

"But I didn't want to, Shaarvan. I am yours. Please let me come to you."

"No. I forbid it."

"Why?"

"Because I love you, Sha . . ."

I was restless in the daytime. I could barely sit down. I began to take long walks. Thal walked with me at times, but I felt guilty, knowing he'd rather be working on his studies. When I said so, Thal assured me that every astronomer enjoyed exploring new planets. It was sweet of him, but he didn't have to accompany me. Spelon and the others usually walked with me each day. They did not seem to object to our daily walks, although I moved as slowly as a sleepy mud lizard.

I did enjoy the occasions when Thal walked with me. His mind was very clever, and he always told me things I didn't know. He told me stories of other planets and the adventures he'd had there. He taught me about the plants we passed and showed me several medically useful ones. I picked some of them, just in case we needed them, but Thal laughed and reminded me that Shapechanger never got sick.

One day, on our walk, we uncovered a wild strand of bilberries. They were ripe for the picking. We crammed a bunch of them into our mouths greedily and then called to the others so we could all harvest the berries. Later, Thal showed us how to dry them, and we mixed them with the wild mena root and made cakes that were left out in the sun to dry.

Another day, our explorations took us to a rainbow-covered waterfall. The water was crystal clear, bubbling over the boulders at the bottom. We sat for a long time, admiring it. I told Thal about the day I'd turned into a mermaid with transition fever. He laughed and looked so sad that I pretended to once more be that mermaid. We found a soft patch of grass to savor his mermaid.

I cared for Thal as I cared for the other three Shapechanger. Each one I held special in my heart. I loved them all in their own different ways. It just wasn't in the same manner in which I loved Shaarvan. Shaarvan was life itself, the spark of the divine. Shaarvan was the other half of me, and our togetherness was a wholeness I couldn't replicate with Thal.

I should not have tried to sort out my thoughts there beside that sparkling water. Thal was too tied to me. I saw again that my thoughts had hurt him and, all my mermaid stunt was wiped away.

"Oh, Thal," I said. "I'm sorry. I do love you." I buried my head on his chest, and he held me, his arms wrapped tightly around my body.

"Thalia," he said. "You have given me some of the best moments of my life. If Shaarvan were here today offering what you and I have shared, I would accept you as my Second once again. To know your joy in life, your curiosity, the way you embrace each moment with delight, and our joinings — I have no regrets, my dear.

"Do you recall the day I first bonded you? You stood there quivering beside me, obedient to Shaarvan's will but wanting nothing more than to run and hide. I treasured you even then. There was a specialness I felt inside you, and I craved it. I coveted you, my best friend's wife. I felt guilt over it, but I was helpless to throw off my desire for you."

I fidgeted, embarrassed by his words. I attempted to break away from the arm, anchoring me to this story.

"No, Thalia. I want you to hear this," Thal demanded.

I sighed and dropped my eyes.

"Do you remember when I touched your body to seal you to me? My fingers burned your skin, and I saw your pain. I felt it, too, but I could not have stopped my hand from traveling you. Your skin was as soft as the petals of a flower and smooth. It curved in luscious ways. My fingers came alive to you, and then, as if a thousand agonies at your breast were not great enough, I slipped inside your inner, secret world and discovered that the skin of your body was not the softest part of you."

I felt my face grow hot and knew I was blushing.

"Oh, Thalia, how adorable you are," he said. He kissed my lips and chuckled. "I am not yet done, my dear. I want you to understand. You see, that day when my finger explored you, did you know that you feel like a combination of silk and velvet inside . . . ?"

I couldn't hear any more of this. Again, I attempted to stand up and dash away.

"Thalia!" Thal's hand on my arm restrained me.

"Please, Thal. I don't mean to hurt your feelings, but when you talk like that, I can't sit still. Don't you understand?"

"You are not Terran anymore, Thalia. You must listen through Shapechanger ears."

I didn't think I could get up by myself anyway, and Thal's hand demanded that I stay. What choice did I have?

Thal ruffled my hair and kissed my forehead. Then, his hand dropped down to rest on unborn Thandar.

"Shapechanger can feel a calling inside them when a woman fulfills their needs. You sent out that calling, Thalia. Your perfect body thrilled me, but that was not all there was to it. There is something in you more special than any woman I have ever known. We are a match, you and I."

"But . . ."

He laid his finger over my mouth and silenced me.

"That day, my malehood grew harder than the nail that drives into a wooden plank, my darling, and I wanted you more than the air I breathe. I would have given everything I owned for just one taste of your sweet nectar and to push my throbbing ache inside you. I would have given life itself."

"But I was Shaarvan's!"

I had forgotten the silence command, yet Thal didn't react to my disobedience. "I know," he said. "And I thought I would never have you, but my desire was still there."

I dropped my eyes and stared down at a single blade of grass. Its point held no sharpness. I plucked it and brought it up to my nose to smell.

Thal shook his head, smiled down at me, and took the blade. Then, he lifted up my chin and kissed me. "It was more than the passion of a moment, Thalia. You were not just a vessel for my ardent need. I craved your essence, and if I could not have it all, I would have been willing to take your body and your mind and revel in that closeness."

I removed his hand from my chin and looked back down. I did not want to hear this story of how Thal had lusted for me while I belonged to Shaarvan. And I resented his forcing me to hear it.

"My story bothers you. You are still shy after all this time of my possession. Do you know how that drives a Shapechanger to stamp you with his claim? Ah, your eyes, Thalia — I could write a book of what I read in your eyes."

Thal lifted up my hand and kissed it, careful not to stir the embers of my desire.

"I know you so well now, my heart's desire. I no longer need your eyes to tell me what you feel. Your emotions are in every pore of you — open, trusting, loving. You are the warmth that every Shapechanger seeks."

Thal turned my hand over, and his lips dipped into my palm. The warm breath of him made my skin tingle in anticipation. His eyes watched me, and he smiled. Then, his tongue descended on my palm. The touch made me gasp.

"The wonder of you is that you feel Shapechanger magic so quickly. I have only to think about it, and you know my thought. I have known no other as receptive."

His hand dropped down to play with my breast. I whimpered my submission. He took my hand down to feel his hardness.

"I am ready for you, my Thalia. I am always ready. My poor tool is hard day in and out for your body. It never seems to be totally appeased, but it is used to being ignored. It will wait. I shall finish telling you my story.

"The day I bonded you — afterward, I would not wash the finger that had plunged within you. The essence of you was on it, like a trophy I had earned. It was the richest perfume, and I floated within its scent.

"So it was that when Shaarvan called me to him, I still harbored the smell of you on me. I feared his anger, but he only laughed."

"He knew how you felt — and he laughed!"

Thal nodded. " 'She has captured you, too,' Shaarvan said. And believe me, Thalia, he read all that I was feeling because I opened up to him. I did not want there to be any lies between us."

"And he didn't care?"

"He knew I was honorable, Thalia. It is not wrong for a male to covet someone's wife. It is only aberrant if he reacts to it."

I wasn't sure if I agreed with that, but Thal wasn't asking for my opinion.

He must have read my thoughts. His lips twisted up, and he chuckled again.

"I forget how young you are, my little wife. You still have so much to learn.

"But I was telling you about my conversation with Shaarvan, and I suppose that I was feeling guilty for how I felt about you and for not having removed the smell of you. I tried to explain to Shaarvan. 'Forgive me,' I said to him. 'Allow me to carry Shaara's memory and the fragrance of her. It is all I shall ever have. She is yours in body, soul, and heart.'

"Shaarvan's eyes had grown even sadder then, Thalia. I thought I had wounded him, but he held up his hand and stopped my words before I could again beg for his forgiveness. He took a great, heavy, soulful gasp of air. I had never seen him like he was that day. But with that will of iron, he stilled himself to go on.

" 'She is my soul, my heart, and my love,' he told me. 'She is my life. I shall only be half-alive without her beside me, but I cannot take her with me to Altar. I can hide from Thenos, but she cannot. She is not yet trained.

" 'You must be her husband, Stegthal. A part of me dies in asking this. I cannot picture her with another, but I have chosen you, my friend, because you will be good to her. She needs great patience. She is rebellious and stubborn. She will not understand your husbanding of her. I am positive you will have to take her forcefully.

" 'She will ask a million questions. Do not answer them all. She is so very young.'

"Shaarvan sighed again and looked off into some inner thought. 'You know she was owned for a while by a fool. He beat her with the pain stick without reason. Try not to beat her, Stegthal. Often, she has driven me to great rages, but words crush her more than punishment. Win her, and she will try to please you.'

"He placed his hand on my arm as if for strength. 'Stegthal, she knows to obey you, but I shall not explain the ceremony to her. She is too intuitive. Her Powers grow. Be careful what she reads from you. Let her stay innocent and loving. Cherish her curiosity. It is her nature to seek answers. That is why I entrust her to you. Allow her to grow and nurture her gently.'

"He turned away, and when he looked up again, his voice was sterner. 'Spelon is next if you . . . Watch him. He feels the pull of her more strongly than he should, and I have seen her unknowingly capture a man by the look in her eye.' "

"I have never . . ."

"Thalia, be silent," Thal chided me. "I know you want to hear Shaarvan's words, but I cannot give them to you if you keep interrupting."

I nodded.

"He continued. 'Keep Shaara safe, and guard Shaarac. He, too, is my life. She will mother him well, but he will need males to foster his growth. Be firm with her there.

" 'It is Altarian law that I must right what Thenos has destroyed. It sends me spinning back into a complicated web of his making. It is highly possible I may never return. Thenos has already attempted to kill me several times, but if I survive, I shall return for her, no matter how long it takes.'

"I gave Shaarvan my word to protect you and to make you mine.

"But as I left him, Shaarvan cried out like a wounded beast, 'I shall return for her, Stegthal, when it is finished. You will give her to me, then.'

"It was a command, not a question, he issued me, but I answered. 'When you return, Shaara is yours.'

"How hard the words grind me now, Thalia. You are my life, my soul, my blood, but to you, I am still only the babysitter."

"Thal, I love you, too." Tears rolled down my cheeks, but I could say no more.

The waterfall continued to babble in its water frolic. The fragrance of crushed grass still permeated the air, along with the almost vanilla scent of the prickly green reeds that sheltered the area. Overhead, the clouds were puffballs, and the background sky was almost as blue as the spring in front of me. But my vision was blurry, and my nose was congested. I was aware, but not aware, lost in the pain of Thal's confession. Breathing grew painful.

Thal patted my hand. "It is right for you to be faithful to Shaarvan, my dear. Do not feel guilty for it, but it rips at my insides now that you are with him each night. You are renewing your soul bindings, leaving me behind already."

"They are only words we share, Thal. We can't touch."

"And you and I can touch but share only the shallowest of soul bindings. And so it is, my dear. And none of us may change it."

I reached out and touched Thal's face. I understood now why he had told me his story. I was grateful. I needed to hear that Shaarvan would be coming back, but I also understood the sadness in Thal's eyes.

I leaned forward and touched my lips to Thal. My kiss turned to need, and the afternoon progressed most pleasantly, although Thandar restricted us.

Thenos

Curse them! They have taken my princess from the planet where I felt her call. She was there. I instructed Chaslow precisely. But when he arrived, she was gone. They have stolen her away again. Those worms!

Chaslow tells me there were numerous signs of habitation and domestic plantings. He found the bedroom where she had lain while I spoke with her. If only she had still been there, eager and ready for me.

Chaslow found long hairs in the bedding that must have been hers. The pillow where her head lay was molded still to her indent. I bid Chaslow to take the hair and the pillow and carry them to me. When I see Chaslow again, I shall have that part of my princess. I shall lay my head against the softness where her head lay and breathe in the scent of her. Perhaps I shall sleep with the pillow wedged against my body, the hair dangling across my chest, but wisps of hair and a used pillow are not enough. I need all of her.

I shall track her down personally and seize her. She will be mine. Why do the others waste my time? Do they not know that in the end, she will belong to me? They must see that. Is it not written in the stars?

Why did they leave Deadstar? How could they have known that I had a Shapechanger in pursuit of them? How could they have left so quickly? And why?

I came to Shaara disguised as Shaarvan. Could she have seen through my illusion? She could not have had the Power to do that. Her thoughts were of Shaarvan. Her words were soft and loving. She was convinced I was her husband. I know she believed the illusion. She is only a woman. She could not have sensed the difference.

She told me nothing when I probed her in her sleep, but she was as open as she has always been. She still cannot bar herself from a Shapechanger. I have seen that. She is as untrained as when I first met her. Yet, there was a change in her. Could it have been the babe in her womb? Could he have strengthened her in some way? I have heard of such. I think it is the most possible explanation.

I know what they call her now. She has been renamed. Of course, they would try to hide her inside a renaming. Thalia. I do not like it at all. Strange how I had never thought about my renaming of her. She was always "princess" to me, but certainly, I must give her a proper name. She will not be Shaara or Thalia. I shall call her Thenosa. Yes, the name has a rhythm to it. Thenosa will suit her well. Princess Thenosa and all will bow before her beauty. Princess Thenosa she will be from henceforth.

And the son she bears . . . he shall be called Thenon. I shall have carvings made, and the great hall will be filled with them. Perhaps I shall add it to her throne. Yes, why not? Princess Thenosa — and I shall have a small chair made for my son, Prince Thenon.

The time is coming. I can feel it. I shall root out the resistance, and then my royal family will be safe beside me in this great hall. And the dirt crawlers will surround us, flinging themselves down to the ground where they belong. And their voices will be all that we hear. They will be crying out their allegiance to my family. I shall rule forever, and my little princess, Princess Thenosa, will be at my side, with her innocent smile, her teeth white and pure and dainty, and she will smile into my eyes and beg for my caresses.

Again, my sword is ready, but I will not visit a woman today. My organ shrivels at the sight of any woman who is not my princess. My sword will wait for Princess Thenosa.

Chapter Two

Thalia

Time had wings that rode the wind. I measured its flight by the circumference of my belly, yet I still had not told Shaarvan that I carried Thal's child.

One day, Thal exploded over my omission. "It shames you that you bear my child. What love will you offer this second babe?"

Guilt hit me, yet I answered him truthfully. "I will love this child equally."

"No, you will turn your back and walk away from him because he is not your beloved's seed."

"Thal," I said, and my tears flowed unceasingly, but for the first time, I doubted my certitude. Could Thal be right? Would I hold it against our child that he was conceived before I was able to love his father? I mentally shook my head. That was not possible. The baby inside me did not deserve such doubts. Of course, I would love him.

But then I remembered how Thaarac had not been seeded in love. Shaarvan had impregnated me without a choice in the matter and all I'd felt for my husband during that time was hatred and fear, but I had still loved Thaarac.

"It was not like you think, Thal. I loathed Shaarvan at first. He was cruel, and he mocked me. He made me feel stupid. While I was undergoing what you males call 'training,' Shaarvan allowed strange men to touch me, and he made me parade before them like I was a robot with no feelings at all.

He abused me in every way. Yet, at night, he drove me mad with desire, and I could not refuse his every wish. But, Thal, what you do not know is that, then, when I first discovered I was pregnant with Thaarac, love for Shaarvan was not within me.

"Shaarvan took me to Altar, and at times, only at times, he began to be kind. I learned to obey him, but it was hard. One day, I attempted to save my planet of origin from the woman trade, and Shaarvan said I betrayed the Shapechanger in my actions. I thought Shaarvan would kill me for doing so, but he chose instead to make me Shapechanger in the Old Way.

"I was only a twentyTide from giving birth, yet Shaarvan frightened me with his Saberey, and then his claws raked my skin with gouges from wrist to elbow — three gouges on each arm. The pain of it, Thal, was more than I could bear. I asked for death, but Shaarvan would not grant that.

"The gouges in my arm, all that pain — they were nothing compared to the agony to come. There was a salve Shaarvan healed me with. The pain of its application and the burning — like acid against my skin — were worse than anything I had experienced before. Shaarvan held me down with the weight of his body. I don't think there was any pain killer in that salve. My wounds kept me awake night and day with the torture of the unceasing sting.

"Then, the fever drove me through the forests of transition. Shaarvan brought me through it, but I was terrified of him then. I trembled whenever he looked in my direction. Not even with a Pass later with Isandor, who beat me until the bruises colored my skin, did

I quake and fear so greatly. Believe me, Thal, there was no love between Shaarvan and me. Not then.

"I don't know how Shaarvan gained my love, but throughout my pregnancy, there was little of it. Yet, I loved Thaarac from the first. Do not fear that I shall short Thandar. You have been far kinder than Shaarvan. If love were fostered in the gentleness of caring, my love for Thandar would be far greater than for Thaarac. But I think a mother loves all her children equally. Is that not true?"

Thal smiled at me and kissed my hand, but he did not have a chance to speak. I continued without his answer.

"You believe I have withheld this child from Shaarvan. You are right. I have been a coward. If you wish, I shall tell Shaarvan the next time we speak."

Thal waited a moment as if to see if I were finished. We were sitting on the couch in the main room. The tale had broken me, withered me into a sobbing mess. Thal wiped my tears with the hem of his shirt. His arms pulled me nearer for a gentle hug.

Then, not content that I was close enough, he dragged me into his lap. His arms enfolded me, swallowing me into the depths of his large, muscled body. He fitted my head against his neck, half-smothering me with his love, but I needed that.

Telling the story of the Saberey transition had ripped me raw, reopening the horrors I'd lived through, revealing the weaknesses inside me and the terrible ache that still lay deep inside me.

"A Shapechanger's training from the female's side is not a pretty picture, my dear. I have heard the pain of the Old Way killed more than half the women, but the rest were strong in the Power. It explains a lot about you, Thalia. It reminds me that you are not bonded by mere love to Shaarvan. You were melded into one from the pain and by the Saberey.

"I am sorry that I doubted you about our son. I shall not command you in this. What is between a husband and his wife cannot be interfered with, but it would make me happier if you told Shaarvan. I do not like feeling like a thief in the night, deceiving him with my seed within your womb."

I sighed. I was afraid to tell Shaarvan. But if I did not, he would be angrier with me for not having told him. He would not forgive me lightly if he found me with a babe in my arms and no prior explanation. Shaarvan was only one part of that, though. The realization of the hurt that I was giving Thal told me that I could not procrastinate another day.

"I will tell him, Thal. What happiness I can bring to you, I owe you, my husband."

It came that night that Shaarvan and I could talk. He knew immediately that I was hesitating over something.

Tell me, Shaara, he ordered.

You forced me to wed Thal against my will, I reminded him.

Yes, because it was best for you.

I have not told you . . .

What Shaara?

I carry his son.

A flash of pain crested Shaarvan's eyes. I could not see it, of course, but I felt it in my heart. Yet, Shaarvan's words were gallant.

I am glad for him, Shaara.

Oh, Shaarvan, I wish the baby were yours.

He is my love, a brother to Shaarac. That is good.

You are not angry with me?

How could I be angry with you when the decision was not yours? It was Stegthal's right.

Thank you, Shaarvan. I was so afraid that you would not want me, knowing this . . .

That is foolish, my wife. Our love is forever. Have you forgotten?

No, but I feared that you . . . When will we be together?

I would be with you now if I could. I love you, my soulmate, with every beat of my heart. It still whispers, Shaara, Shaara . . .

I am yours . . .

Shaarvan

My poor Shaara. How sad she sounds. I cannot ask her if Thal pleases her. It would not be proper, yet I feel the depth of her unhappiness. Is it only because she and I are separated? I am sure my old friend would not treat her harshly. He loved her from their first encounter.

I worry over this child she carries. Shaara is fully transitioned now. The birth will be easier for her. But she is so small, and if I had not summoned the Old Ones before, I think she would not have survived the birthing of Shaarac.

Later, I spoke with Pathe. He assured me that Shaara's body was well-provisioned for Shapechanger birthing, but I recalled too vividly the feel of her beneath me and the smallness of her bones. Stars! Let Stegthal's son be smaller than Shaarac. Let her ease the child out as easily as a cubbing. Let her not feel all the pain and fear she felt that first time.

Old Ones, watch over my Shaara, I cried out in the night when I was alone once more. I received no response. The Saberey rarely responded to such pleas, but I knew they would hear me. That somewhat soothed my soul. Shaara was a Trendacons, part of their pack. Surely, that would matter to them.

I felt a vague kind of reaction, an almost imperceptible caress. It was the reassurance that they would watch out for her. They were now aware of my concern and alerted me to her need. It would not matter where she was. I knew they would help.

I have never asked my wife where she and the others are. I would not chance Thenos' receptivity. I hope they are far enough away that my brother will cease his searching. Why must he continue this obsession anyway? Does he not have an abundance of fresh girls delivered each sevenTide? I pray that one of them will take his sick preoccupation away from Shaara.

Our spies told us of the bombing of the nursery on Westla. My guilt was heavy for the sons of so many Westlans, yet I could not help the joy I felt that Shaarac was not among them. Hide away, my family. I shall end this battle before much longer. Already, Thenos' forces weaken.

I shall never ask where Shaara has been taken, but there are things that I can surmise. I am sure there are trees and greenery nearby. Shaara's soul is too calm for desert or barren soil. I think she has pets, too. Her temperament has a need for them. I know from things Shaara has said that they share the planet with no others.

It is probably an unlisted world and one out of the space net, yet I think that Stegthal would not have taken her to an unscouted planet. That would have been too risky. Therefore, I have clues that I could use to locate her, but I shall not. I care only that she and Shaarac are safe.

Thalia

Thandar arrived in the wee hours of the night. He was early but strong and healthy. He cried out lustily. But when I put him on my breast, he had little interest. His little wrinkled face creased up into a yawn, and he slept.

Tenderly, I checked him over. The tiny little fingers and toes seemed unbelievably perfect. He was not as beautiful as Thaarac had been, but he was mine, and I would love him.

Thal had delivered Thandar and cleaned me up afterward. I was embarrassed by such intimacy. He had seen me at my worst. How could he still love me?

Thal chuckled at my thought. "In ancient times, Thalia, men always delivered their wives. It was a sacred right and privilege. What is more fitting than that the seed I placed inside your womb, I should help ease out? And there was no ugliness in the birth, my dear, only great beauty. You have honored me so enormously with this tiny babe. I shall be forever grateful for my son."

I had not walked the forest and given birth to my cub as I had done with Shaarvan. Thal had not needed to take me there. He had been right. Thandar's birth was far easier than Thaarac's had been.

I held out my hand to Thal, and there was a new bond between us. Thal was a good Shapechanger. I was glad to be his wife. And I was happy that Thandar had come into the world knowing his father's gentle touch.

We rested for a while as Thandar slept. My eyes were heavy, and I think I dozed. When Thandar awakened not long after, he loudly made his desire known. His little face reddened with his utter unhappiness, and his wail was like a squeaky little door. Thal placed his son's soft little head at my breast. It was Thal's finger that urged the nipple into Thandar's mouth, and my husband's eyes glowed with happy pride as his son slurped greedily at my breast.

Later, the others came to see the new arrival to our troop. They gathered all around me, and their smiles were radiant. Little Thaarac patted my arm, Tenor and Thedar congratulated me, and Spelon brought me a bouquet of freshly picked flowers.

"You are well?" Spelon kept asking. He had wanted Thal to take me to the ship to deliver Thandar and was very upset that Thal had not.

"I am fine, Spelon. Please do not fuss," I said.

"You cleaned her up properly?" he demanded of Thal. "You are sure. You inspected . . ."

Thal took him aside and talked with him awhile, but, in the end, the others had to escort Spelon out because he made such a nuisance of himself.

Truthfully, I was quite content to see them go. My eyes were sagging, and I was jealous of Thandar, asleep in my arms. Thal must have understood. He left me alone and went back to his studies. I was probably asleep before he'd opened the first book.

The new little brother pleased Thaarac. He held him in his arms the next day. I fretted that he would drop his brother, but Thal flashed me the "no argument" sign, and I bit my lip. Still, Thal hovered beside Thaarac, and no parent could have been more protective.

After a moment, Thal told our toddler that baby Thandar must be fed by his mommy. Thaarac had no memory of nursing, and although he wished to believe his father, he found it difficult to accept that there was milk inside a woman.

"Thaarac, did you never see your mother's breasts?" Thal asked him.

I shot Thal dark looks that he ignored. Once more, he flashed a warning that I was not to obstruct the lesson. When Thal reached inside my dress, pulling the material away so Thaarac could see, I came the closest to arguing since Westla. My hand tugged at the material covering me. Thal swatted it away and flashed a Second Warning.

I was furious, but I didn't dare challenge. Second Warning was a serious matter. Thal continued to ignore my flashing eyes and went on with his instruction. "Giving milk is the purpose for a woman's breasts. Nature is very clever. A woman grows the baby here and feeds it there. The male plants the seed with his tool. That seed grows into a baby. Then the male takes care of his wife and sons."

"See bweasts. No milk."

I was so uncomfortable I flashed another sign of protest. Once more, Thal disregarded it.

"All right, Thaarac. Get up in bed with Mommy and taste her milk. You will see then."

Once again, my fingers flashed. Thal took my hand and held it still. He dropped a kiss on my fingers and laid them to the side, then chuckling at my inhibitions, he lifted Thaarac and placed him on the bed beside me. I took the opportunity to hug Thaarac. My son resisted my embrace, and Thal's sharp "Let him go" told me that neither male appreciated my interruption of the lesson.

Thal's eyes, when they met mine, were no longer laughing. There was even more threat in them. "Do not interfere, Thalia. I shall not warn you again."

"Take your mother's breast in your mouth and suck, Thaarac."

Thaarac did as he was told. He drank for a moment, tasted it, and swallowed.

"Good mommy. Feed baby." He patted me on the cheek, jumped off the bed, and ran off to play. I watched him and then looked at Thal, amazed.

His eyes softened, and he sat down beside me on the bed. "I did not wish to be severe with you, my dear, but you were very defiant."

"I am sorry."

His hand caressed my face. "Do not defy me again, Thalia. I do not wish to punish you, but I shall do so if it is needed."

I dropped my eyes. I knew he would not accept an explanation.

"That is correct. Your prior cultural indoctrination is of no importance. You are Shapechanger now. It is the father who raises the son. I shall allow no interference from you."

I started to question him, but his finger blocked my speaking. "You may love your sons, Thalia. Tell them stories, sing them songs, answer their queries, but the raising of them belongs to the Shapechanger males of the family."

"On Earth . . ." I waited to see if Thal would allow me to speak. He nodded. "On Earth, it is the woman who mainly raises the child."

"I know. Shaarvan told me."

"You didn't tell me that you discussed Thaarac as well."

"A Shapechanger does not need to tell everything he knows to his wife."

"It might help the wife to understand."

"A wife does not need to understand, only to obey."

"Thal, sometimes I do not like Shapechanger logic."

"I know."

Spelon

Thal was foolish to have forced Thalia to give birth on this primitive sphere. She is fragile, unused to such hardships. Does he know that? She was lucky the babe came so easily. I have seen women die in the giving of new life.

I took the nursery sack that she had expelled and inspected it thoroughly. It looked intact, but only one spot torn away and left inside a woman could bring on her death. Why does Thal refuse my request to take her back to the ship? I could carry her the entire way. It would be worth it to have the ship's computers check Thalia over.

I have spoken to the others, but they will not interfere. They agree with me that it would be worth the trouble, but they will not go against Thal's decision. Are we not responsible for the girl? Is it not our duty to oversee Thal's governance of her? I do not understand why they permit such a risky decision.

He is a stubborn male, this mysterious Shapechanger. I do not like him.

Thalia

Thal made me stay in bed for a week. I wasn't ill, and I resented my imprisonment. Tenor, Thedar, and Spelon all came and entertained me, but I wanted up and out.

There were chittering thebas and birds twittering in the trees, flowers growing, and trees bursting with buds of sweet fragrance. It irked me to have to lie there, shut away from it.

I complained to them all, but no one would commiserate with me. Even Thaarac said, "Daddy say better soon."

Thaarac handed me a bouquet of wild flowers. I thanked him and said, "Tell Daddy I am better **now**."

Only moments later, Thal came storming in. He shut the door and then sat down on the bed beside me. "I think you are feeling rebellious," he stated. He said nothing more but sat there, looking like a doctor giving bad news.

I could not meet his eyes. I could feel his exasperation with me, but I was frustrated, too. I didn't need to stay in bed, and he was being mean to insist on it.

When I remained silent, Thal sighed heavily and spoke. "You have complained to everyone, Thalia. We are tired of it. I assume you have even grumbled to Shaarvan. What did he say?"

I was wishing I didn't always have to be truthful.

"Thalia?"

"He said you were right and that I must obey."

Thal shook his head as if that just confirmed what he thought. "You have been told to stop your complaints. I am especially disappointed that you would involve Thaarac in what you presume to be an arguable issue."

Tears were brimming in my eyes. I felt like the villain everyone "booed" and hissed at in an old-fashioned melodrama.

"I'm sorry, Thal," I told him, hanging my head in shame.

Thal watched for a moment. Then he raised my chin and saw the tears flowing.

"Do not cry, my little one. This, too, will pass, and the sun will still be in the sky, the flowers will wait for you, and the birds will still be singing just as long and loud. Be patient, my dear."

He lay down with me and watched me nurse Thandar. Thandar's little fists jerked in motion with his slurping noises. The baby was so adorable now. The redness had gone away, and he was making up for being early with a spurt of growing. Every so often, Thandar would stop and look at me, his eyes so pale a blue that I wondered if they'd ever change to gray.

"Your son grows stronger each day, Thal," I told my husband. "Already, his hand clenches strongly. You have to pry his fist away from your finger with both hands."

Thal laughed proudly. Thandar jerked. His eyes turned to his father. Thal stretched out his finger and let Thandar grab it. The eyes never left his father's face.

We were still admiring our beautiful son when Thaarac entered the room with my bondmates. He had a poem to tell us, he said proudly.

Thedar and Tevor said most of it, and Thaarac yelled a word here and there that he remembered, but he was bursting with pride. I thought Spelon, who couldn't seem to recite it, would weep before it ended.

My mommy and daddy

Have given to me

A little baby brother.

I will play with him,

And teach him songs,

And show him how to walk.

But I have to wait

Til he grows a bit

Cause now he only sleeps.

I clapped when he was finished, and Thaarac looked at me strangely.

"No, Mommy! Be quiet."

The males gathered all around me and started laughing, but I knew I had hurt Thaarac's feelings.

"Come here, Thaarac," I said to him. He came running and flung himself into my arms, although Thal had called out for him to be gentle. I hugged Thaarac and said, "I am sorry, my son. Sometimes I forget that I am no longer in the place where I grew up. There, they clapped like this," and I showed Thaarac how we had clapped on Earth. "That meant that we liked something very, very much," I explained.

"OK, Mommy. OK. Spel say women 'alwys' make noise!"

I glared at Spelon, but he only shrugged at me.

"Thal, this is training?"

"Sometimes women do make an awful lot of noise."

The males were smiling broadly, but they didn't meet my eyes. The rest of the visit was brief but pleasurable. It was nice to see them all.

Being grounded in my room became easier after that. Thal and the others frequently came in and gathered around to talk or sing chants.

They taught Thaarac his lessons in my room. When they were teaching, I had to promise not to speak, no matter what I wanted to say. I agreed, but sometimes it was terribly hard to be silent!

Every so often, Thal would stop the lessons and order everyone to move outside. I would protest, saying that I had not spoken.

"It is not a punishment," Thal would tell me. "It is that sometimes there are things you may not hear."

"There are things you tell a toddler that I'm not supposed to hear?"

Thal didn't answer. His hands began to stroke me. Each day after that, he handled me and brought me to fulfillment, but he would not allow me to touch him, nor would he take me for the twentyTide that he had declared I needed to recover fully.

"Why may I not pleasure you as you do me?" I asked.

"It is forbidden."

"Why?"

"Enough, Thalia."

"But I have touched you . . ."

He rose up, growling at me. "Spelon is right. Women do make too much noise."

For the rest of that day, I was left alone. I didn't cry. My anger flared. Shapechanger males were so unfair! That night, I was still angry, and I turned my back to Thal.

"A wise woman remembers well the Primary," Thal said. There was warning in his voice and in his words.

I lay there, perhaps five seconds, in stony silence, then I let out a whimper and turned back to him. Thal's eyes were still watching me.

"Good girl," he said. "I did not wish to beat the mother of my son."

I stared into his eyes, appalled by the seriousness of Thal's voice. His eyes were still watching me, and they were not smiling.

At last, he pulled me towards him. I didn't dare move away, but it was a long time before I could close my eyes.

The next day, all was as before. The men taught Thaarac. I listened and admired my sons, and I nursed Thandar. Then, in the afternoon, Thal sent them out. Once more, he placed Thandar in his crib and came to me. His lips met mine. I didn't fight Thal, but I was nervous as a virgin. He had to use many patterns on me.

"Must I web you today?" He was joking, but I was too frightened to see.

"No!" I cried out in alarm. I hated the paralyzed feeling of the webs.

He sat up and studied me. "What is it, Thalia? A nightmare? Does Thenos search for you again?"

I shook my head, but I was trembling. Thal stroked my hair and stared at me in puzzlement. I tried to block his probe, but I had no skill that would stand up to a Shapechanger lord. A moment later, he found the answer.

"Thalia, you challenged me yesterday. That is over and done with. You have no need to fear me today."

"But I didn't mean to challenge you, and you were going to beat me," I told him as I wiped a tear off my cheek.

"How often have I beaten you?"

I had to think hard. I was sure it had been many times, but I could only remember the time when Thal had first taken me. "Once?"

He nodded. "Nor do I wish to increase that number. Only disobedience or disrespect would cause me to strike you, Thalia. Now, relax. You have nothing to fear from me."

It took Thal a long time to reassure my body of that. When I tensed up, Shapechanger magic didn't always work well. We were both worn out by the time Thal achieved his will.

When Thal was done, I was able to relax. He held me then and talked of the stars. His hand soothed my skin and gentled me. Once more, he claimed my lips, but he demanded nothing of me. I relaxed into the sweetness as he took away my fear.

I was allowed to go outside at the end of that Tide. I was so excited I am sure that joy was written across my face. I know it was reflected in the smiles of everyone around me.

Happy mommy in the sun

Sitting on the grass

Loving baby, loving me

Happy mommy in the sun.

Thaarac recited with the help of his father.

I opened my arms to my son and kissed his face until he grew wild and pushed me away.

"Who's the poet?" I asked him before he dashed out of sight.

"Daddy," he yelled back. Then, he was off to share with the others. Thal sheepishly stood there watching me. I smiled up at him, and he came towards me and planted a kiss on my forehead.

A sudden growl alerted us to the approach of a Shapechanger in full change. It came charging at Thal. I changed, as did my husband. We both stood there, growling at the intruder. A sea of heavy dark yellow buzzed about us. Rotten garbage scent flooded the air from our anger.

The strange cat halted his charge, puzzled. Then he changed back into human form. In that instant, I knew him.

I reverted to my normal form and went running towards him, proudly remembering my dress. I flung myself into the Shapechanger's arms and kissed him on the cheek. It wasn't Shaarvan, but it was my second best, my love, Tren.

"You did it! You became a Shapechanger," I cried out, hugging him madly.

He wasn't fighting me this time. His arms surrounded me. His lips touched my forehead. "Shaarvan's man, Targone, gave me no choice. But the transition was worth it, Shaara."

Rain on concrete, the odor of happiness — I laughed and hugged Tren harder.

At that moment, Thal ripped me out of Tren's arms. My husband was back in his human form, too, but he was growling deeply. He tossed me into Spelon's hold. Spelon shoved me into Tenor's arms and waded into the fight raging between Tren and Thal.

"No! Don't," I began screaming, struggling to get free of Tenor. "Stop it! He's my friend!"

Spelon looked back at me and roared his displeasure. "We saw the kind of friend, Thalia."

When everyone had had their punch and Tren was unconscious, Thal stopped them. "Enough," he said. "Spelon, take my wife to the barn and hold her there. I shall deal with her later."

The look Thal gave me made my knees quake. He was angrier than I'd ever seen him. Yellow haze coated him like the thickness under a pollinating Spinon tree.

"Tenor, you go with Spelon. Thedar, let's take this Shapechanger into the house and do some questioning. I want to know exactly how he found us."

"Thal, please, listen to me," I said, sobbing because it had all gone so wrong, and no one would listen.

Spelon tried to drag me away, but my feet were well-planted in the dirt. Thaarac was staring open-mouthed at everything. Thal swooped him up and started to carry him away, but our son was so frightened by the sudden violence he began screaming, "Mommy, Mommy!" His little arms stretched out to me but Spelon was holding me still.

"It's all right, Thaarac. Go with Daddy. Mommy will see you later," I called out.

I turned on Spelon then with all my fury. "Stop it! Spelon. Take your hands off me. I shall go willingly if . . ."

Spelon didn't give me a chance to finish. He jerked me close to his body in preparation for a Shapechanger crossover, but I swung a kick at him, which he avoided. Without saying anything, he tossed me over his shoulder. His hand came down on my rump with a slap of warning. I snarled, but I didn't fight him anymore.

Spelon carried me into the barn and dumped me into the hay. "Start talking, Thalia. Who is that Shapechanger?"

"Now you ask me!" I yelled. I was far beyond the ability to control my tongue and temper. Spelon always made me so spitting mad!

He raised his hand to strike me.

"No, Spelon," Tenor said, halting the hand. "She is Thal's to discipline." Tenor began to channel his Shapechanger force at me.

I shook my head to clear it. I was angrier now than before. Even Tenor doubted me?

"You don't need to hit me or to use your force. I will gladly tell you. I've been trying to tell you!"

"Then hurry it up," Spelon growled.

"It's Tren. He's the commoner who owned me on Freinana, the one who called the Shapechanger so Shaarvan could find me. He's Shaarvan's friend and mine."

"He is not a man. He is a Shapechanger. Explain that. And you were much more than friendly to him," Spelon roared.

"We were bonded, he and I. I had no memory of Shaarvan, you see, and Targone was going to force me to be his wife . . ."

"Who's Targone?" Tenor demanded.

"He was the Shapechanger who came to see if I was truly one of the blood. Please, please, don't let them hurt Tren. He became Shapechanger because Shaarvan forced him to!"

Tenor studied my eyes. Whatever he read there decided him. "I shall tell her story to Thal. Thal might kill the Shapechanger if I don't explain."

Tenor jogged off, leaving Spelon to glare at me.

"Stop it, Spelon," I said angrily.

"You forget yourself, woman."

"Shaarvan would have understood," I said, stamping my foot.

"Shaarvan is not your husband now."

My eyes glared with anger. "Shaarvan will always be my husband."

Spelon flashed a warning at me. It was at Second Level. Any higher and he would beat me or have Thal do so. I lowered my eyes, but my temper didn't cool.

I was worried about what they'd do to Tren. What if they'd already hurt him? I would never forgive my bondmates if they gave Tren a serious injury.

"Shapechanger males are tough," Spelon said, reading my mind. "You had better start worrying about what your *husband* will do to you."

I said nothing, but I was surprised that as angrily as I was staring at the hay, it didn't catch fire.

Thal came in shortly after. I started to run to him, but Spelon barked out, "Stay, woman."

Spelon turned and faced Thal. "Thalia has been argumentative, disobedient, and full of challenge. She is at a Stage 2 warning, but I suggest that she receive full punishment in addition to what you do to her for her brazen behavior with the stranger."

"I see," Thal said. "Thank you for your report, Spelon. You may leave us now."

I kept my head down, eyes on the ground. Nothing Spelon had said was false. I had no defense.

Thal walked towards me. When he stood directly in front of me, I flung myself at his knees and said, "I'm sorry. Forgive me. I deserve to be beaten, but please don't hurt Tren. It was my fault."

Thal's voice, when it came, was cold. "Stand up, Wife. You are Shapechanger."

I stood, but I kept my eyes lowered.

"Look at me."

I obeyed. It was just as I'd feared. There was only a cold hardness in Thal's eyes.

"Tren is still unconscious. The others will not touch him. We will discuss his future later, but the Shapechanger's future does not concern you, Thalia. That is the business of males.

"You will tell me now what transpired to make Spelon so angry."

I did not want to look Thal in the eyes. I was afraid he'd read my avoidance. "I lost my temper," I said.

"Why?"

"I was upset about Tren."

"Thalia, you are lying."

I gasped and looked into Thal's eyes. "Shapechanger cannot lie."

"You have given me a Shapechanger lie. You will tell me exactly what Spelon said to make you flare at him."

I could not avoid the truth. Thal would not tolerate my evasion. "Spelon said that Shaarvan was not my husband anymore."

"That is not correct, is it? Spelon meant that Shaarvan was not here."

"How can a day that starts so perfectly end so rottenly?" I asked.

"A star that explodes can appear normal until the moment it novas, but inside it, there was turmoil for a long time."

Sometimes, I did not understand Thal. He saw my confusion.

"Tren has been searching for you for a manyTide. Spelon has been angry that I am lax with you for as long as we have been bonded. You have been threatening to explode for at least a quarterTide. It all came together — a nova."

"What will you do?"

Thal's hand continued to stroke my cheek, but I knew enough about Shapechanger to know that a caress was not a sign of a pardon.

"I shall collect more information about Tren."

I tried not to show stress over my punishment, but it was difficult not to be concerned. "What will you do to me?"

"Thalia, if I do not punish you, a fine warrior will be insulted. He will accept no less than physical punishment. You are often out of line with your bondmates. They are Shapechanger lords, and you are but a woman — a Powerful one and highly owned — but still, only a female. You must respect them, obey them, and trust their judgment. Is that understood?"

I nodded.

"Strip."

I took off my dress and placed it on a bale of hay. There was a leather piece of harness hanging. It had been brought from Deadstar. Thal unbuckled one section and folded it over his hand.

"You will stand still, or I shall double it, Thalia."

Again, I nodded and braced for the pain.

The strap bit across my legs and buttocks. The pain was like a thousand bee stings. I screamed and sagged to the ground.

"Stand up, Thalia. There will be one on each side."

Once more, Thal lashed out, and again I screamed, then stood frozen, waiting for the pain to stop.

Thal dropped the lash and turned me to face him. His arms enfolded me. "A man sometimes receives twenty to forty of those lashes on his back. The skin tears and bleeds with that many. I was easy with you, my wife, but I think the lash, like the scratches you bear on your arm, will make you remember for a long time. You are not to argue with a Shapechanger male, nor raise your voice, nor struggle when he holds you still."

I nodded and looked down. Thal was still for a long while. What was he thinking about? Was he debating other consequences? Was he thinking about adding more lashes to those he had given me? I couldn't stand the quiet.

"Will you punish me for kissing Tren?" I blurted out.

Thal was silent another moment. I felt him reading me. The touch of his mind in mine was like a breath against my cheek. I did not attempt to block him. There would have been no point.

"You are courageous, my wife," he said, and I knew that he had withdrawn. I sighed and looked up. His eyes were still studying me. Quickly, I looked down again.

"You would rather hear the truth than run and hide from it. That pleases me, Thalia."

He was still gazing down at me. I could feel his eyes, pondering his judgment.

"Your greeting of Tren did not please me," Thal said slowly. "Which means that you broke the Primary . . ."

I did not groan, although my buttocks still stung like fire. The thought of more swats made me want to bolt, but I didn't move. My teeth clenched tightly, but I remained silent. Pride was all I had to withstand the world of the Shapechanger. If Thal decided that I should be punished more, I refused to cower or beg.

Thal pulled me close. His lips touched my forehead lightly. "Yes, you are courageous, my little one," he said, knowing my thoughts as usual. "And I shall not rob you of that pride, not as long as you are free of defiance."

I looked up at him. Defiance? How could Thal think I challenged him?

He chuckled. "I know, Thalia. You did not mean to disobey. Women often do not think with their brains but with their hearts."

Thal was stroking my cheek with his hand, but he had not yet answered my question. What would he do to me? Once more, I looked up.

He nodded. "You broke the Primary, Thalia, but I will not fault you this time. You have been punished enough."

I threw my arms around my husband and kissed his cheek. I hurt, but it could have been a lot worse. Once again, Thal had been patient with me.

He stopped me and held me away from him. Obviously, the lecture part was still not over.

"*This time,* Thalia. Did you listen to that part, my dear?"

I nodded and bit my lip.

"You are duly warned, my wife. If there are any more stray bondmates who come searching for you, if you kiss them, next time, I shall punish you."

Thal was not joking. I nodded my head and dropped my eyes in obedience.

"Good. We must return to the others now. Thandar will be needing you soon."

I started to gather my clothes, but Thal ordered me to be still. He went himself and picked up my dress. He shook it out and picked off stray bits of straw. Then he slipped it down over my lifted arms and head. Leaving my shoes there in the barn, he carried me back to the house.

Spelon

Thal will not be rough with her. He will probably lecture Thalia about comets or solar fires and expect her to figure out what he means by that. I know he will not beat her. He does not have that harshness in him. But what if I am wrong? Would I see her lashed because of what I said?

Perhaps I should go back and tell Thal that I forgive the woman. She is young and impulsive. Had she thought it out, I am sure that Thalia would not have yelled at me. She did not mean to challenge. I know that now. Yet, at the time, my temper . . .

Her temper is like mine, full-breasted and hot. She has not yet learned to harness it. I was like that, too, when I was her age. She should not be punished for the impetuosity of her youth. I must tell Thal that. But, if I do, he will think I am interfering.

I will tell Tenor. He can go to Thal and speak . . .

Yet, Thalia should be punished. She must be taught her role. I shall say nothing. I am sure that Thal will not hurt her.

Thalia

All eyes turned to us as we walked in. Spelon's eyes were full of triumph. I glared at him.

"Thalia," Thal warned me sharply. I lowered my eyes.

"Thalia, you will ask Spelon's forgiveness for your conduct," Thal stated firmly.

I couldn't believe that Thal would make me do that! It was so unfair, like a double punishment. Thal's eyes warned.

I walked up to Spelon with a huge sigh of protest. My eyes were raised, and I knew not to challenge him, but I wasn't going to cower, either. "I ask forgiveness for my disobedience, my . . ."

"Challenge and argumentativeness," Thal supplied.

"I ask forgiveness for my disobedience, my challenge, and my argumentativeness," I said.

Spelon's eyes were intense. I thought for a moment he looked uncomfortable, but his words did not reveal it.

"I accept your apology, Thalia," he said, and there was annoyance in his voice. He might have been about to say something more, but I turned away from him. I had done what was required of me. I didn't have to listen to Spelon's lectures.

"Raise your dress to show him your punishment," Thal ordered from behind me.

"Raise my dress?" I squawked. Thal had really shocked me. I knew nakedness wasn't a taboo for Shapechanger as it was for Terrans, but . . .

"Hold. I shall do it," Thal said.

Thal strode up to me and flashed my buttocks quicker than I could have, but I knew my face was the color of the inside of a red, ripe watermelon. I hid against my husband's shirt.

"You are satisfied?" Thal asked Spelon.

Spelon must have nodded. I didn't hear him speak.

Thal led me into our room. Both Thandar and Thaarac were sleeping. My husband quietly located a jar of salve and rubbed it on my welts. It hurt where he touched, but the stinging eased. It felt nothing like the scratches Shaarvan had given me.

Thal ordered me to lie there, and he woke up little Thandar and brought him to me. I think my husband realized it would be awhile before I was able to sit up and nurse Thandar as I usually did.

When I was finished, I played with Thaarac. He seemed to have forgotten his earlier fright. He didn't question me about it or the command of Thal for me to stay in bed. Thaarac was too much a Shapechanger to be disturbed by such a thing.

It was a couple of hours later that Tren woke up. Thal made him drink something to clear his head, and Spelon and Tenor gathered around to listen to his responses. Thedar had taken Thaarac outside. I wondered if the bondmates had drawn straws and Thedar had gotten the short one.

Tren's eyes were skimming the room as he drank. I knew he was looking for me. When his eyes found me leaning against the wall over in the corner, I felt the force of his regard, but I did not look up. I did not want more trouble for him or for me.

"Why do you not allow Shaara to sit?" Tren demanded angrily.

"She is free to sit or stand as she chooses," Thal said.

Spelon laughed. I would have glared at him, but Thal was watching me too closely. I did spot Tenor giving Spelon an extremely sharp look of annoyance. (I learned later that for a threeTide neither Tenor nor Thedar spoke to Spelon.)

Tren was oblivious to the undertones. He blustered on. "Where is Shaarvan, and why were you kissing Shaara?"

"You are the one who needs to answer questions," Spelon said angrily.

Again, I was careful not to glare at Spelon. Thal's eyes lingered on me once more.

One of Thal's eyebrows had lifted slightly. It meant trouble for someone. I was glad that I'd kept silent as Thal had ordered.

"Spelon," Thal said, turning to look fully at Spelon. "I thank you for your assistance, but I think if only one of us handles the questioning, it will flow more orderly."

Spelon would have argued the point, but Tenor jabbed him in the stomach. The warrior growled like a brown bear, but he didn't react further. Perhaps Spelon had finally tuned into the anger of those around him.

Thal gave Spelon no time to answer. He turned, and said, "Tren, does anyone know where you are or where you were going? This is very important for the life of the woman you call Shaara."

Tren shot another glance at me. I looked down.

"The Old Ones and Tessa sent me. They and Tem all know that I went in search of Shaara, but no one knows where," Tren said, his eyes still boring into me. "I did not know where I was headed. I felt Shaara's pull, and I followed it."

I gasped and looked up. Our eyes met then. I hoped that Tren realized how horrified his statement had made me feel. I glanced at Thal and saw that he was glowering at me. Quickly, I dropped my eyes again, hoping that Thal would not order me to my room.

I felt Thal's appraisal, but he said nothing to me.

"No one followed you, and you came alone?" Thal questioned.

Tren had grown impatient. He shook his head crossly. I knew he wouldn't respond to any more questions before his own questions were answered. Even with the quickness of that one glance, I had seen the stubborn look on his face, one I'd seen often in the casino. His cheekbones might be higher, and his eyes raincloud gray, but he was still Tren.

Thal studied me. I felt his probe. I offered no resistance. He nodded, satisfied.

Tren didn't know what Thal was doing. I could see his face turning back and forth, trying to interpret the look between Thal and me. I wished I could explain, but, of course, I couldn't.

"Shaarvan fights on Altar," Thal told Tren. "His brother, Thenos, began a war there, and Shaarvan was forced to join in. Shaarvan could not take the one you call 'Shaara' with him. She broadcasts if you understand what that means."

Tren shook his head. He was still staring at me as if measuring the changes.

I thought about that. What changes was Tren seeing? Did I look older? Did he still think I was beautiful, as he'd called me once? I was still thin. Motherhood had not changed that. My breasts were fuller, thanks to nursing Thandar. My hair was longer than on Freinana. Isandor had cut it once so that it only reached the midpoint of my back. It hung down now below my waist, still as curly. I had no mirror to see my face. Did I look different? Thal was talking again. I curbed my thoughts.

"Shapechanger use that term to mean a woman who projects her thoughts and emotions without control over them. Shaara — she is called Thalia now — has great Power but little ability to manage it," Thal told Tren.

Thal had relaxed somewhat. He pulled up a chair and sat down beside Tren. "For that reason, Thalia could not be taken to Altar. She would have brought Thenos down on all of them."

I dared another look at Tren. His eyes were still on me. A shock passed through me when I saw his naked longing.

I peeked at Thal, saw warning in his eyes, and quickly bowed my head.

"Since Shaarvan could not take Thalia with him, he was forced to bond her to us. Shaarvan made me Thalia's Second, her husband."

"Husband! What? Shaara, did they tell you that?" Tren demanded, bolting up.

I wanted to respond to him, but Thal had issued the silence command. I continued my appraisal of the wooden floor.

"Both Shaarvan and Thalia were present at the ceremony of bonding, and later, when I became her husband, all of us, including Thalia, attended."

Tren didn't sit back down. He raised his hands and pulled at his hair. "No, I don't — do not — believe it," he yelled.

Spelon was growling again. He shifted into a warrior stance. Thal shook his head at him.

Tren had bolted up, not seeming to notice Spelon's posture. He was looking at Thal, still shaking his head in disbelief. "I saw the two of them together. Shaarvan and Shaara were melded like two fingers of the same hand. Shaarvan would never have left . . ."

I couldn't help my sob. It came out of nowhere, then the tears that followed came faster and faster.

Thal scooted back in his chair and stood up. I heard his steps approaching, and in a moment, he was putting his great, massive arms around me and turning me towards his chest. "Easy, Thalia. I know it hurts," he soothed.

Thal's shirt was wet with my tears before I could quiet myself.

"Holy spit!" Tren cried out. "You have deserted your husband for him?"

That started me off again. I shook with misery. My outpouring of tears seemed to have no end.

I could feel Thal getting angry. I knew his anger was not directed at me, yet the waves of it were overwhelming me. I took in huge gulps of air in an attempt to gain control.

"Please . . ." I said.

Thal didn't wait for me to finish. "Get Tren out of here," he commanded. "Thalia has had enough."

"No," I said between my tears. "Please, Thal, please don't let them hurt Tren. He just doesn't understand."

Thal lifted up my chin and stared into my eyes. I felt his irritation with me then, but he sighed and patted my cheek. "You are right, my wife. They are angry enough to take a few more punches. And Thaarac is outside. Stay here. I shall be right back."

Thal's absence allowed me to regain control, but when he came back, his arms once more surrounded me. "My poor Thalia," Thal said. "It has been a nova day for you. Tomorrow, we shall locate a new star, a more stable one."

He picked me up and carried me to the bed. "Sleep now, Thalia," he ordered me. "Thandar will probably be waking up soon, demanding his next meal."

I hadn't had any lunch, but I didn't care. I closed my eyes and attempted to savor the comfort of the bed. Thal kissed me and stroked my cheek a moment. I kept my eyes closed and pretended I was sleepy. The sweet oblivion of slumber would truly be a welcome respite from all the stress around me. Yet, as I heard Thal's footsteps withdrawing from the room, I knew I wouldn't sleep. I kept seeing Tren's accusing eyes, and the words "You have deserted your husband" kept ringing in my ears.

Tren

I do not understand what I have stumbled into. It is all craziness. Shaarvan could barely stand to let his wife out of his sight on Freinana. To think he would fly away and leave her to another male . . . No, I do not believe that. And if what Thal said is true, why did the Old Ones not tell me so on Westla?

I was told of Shaara's bondmates, but it was never mentioned that one of them was supposed to be husbanding Shaara. So why did they send me to her? Why did Tessa say that I was to guide Shaarvan when my new brother is not even here?

The bondmates have to be lying to Shaara. I know that. Yet, they are Shapechanger. How could they lie? I simply do not understand this nest of squirming snakes.

The one who calls himself Thal is the head of the group. Shaara is frightened of him. I could see that by the way she kept looking at him, checking to see if he was angry with her, her eyes like two Daneb fruits, huge with fear. Thal silenced her before she was able to speak with me. What did Thal fear she would say? What would Shaara have told me?

There is no doubt in my mind that Shaara needs me. That is why I felt her pull. If she has met up with another male who beats her and then mocks her scars, I shall kill him. It is four to one, all of them big, strong Shapechanger, but I have played worse odds.

Poor kid. I wish I were the one putting my arm around her tonight. I would never beat her. I would comfort her and cradle her in my arms. I would brush back her lustrous hair, kiss her fears away, and warm her body. I would take her mind away from Shaarvan . . . and Thal.

Chapter Three

Thalia

Shaarvan. He was once again in the lookout post. *"Tren has come. He said I pulled him to me."*

Good. He will help protect you. Is he a Shapechanger now?

Yes.

I am glad that he is there for you.

But he thinks I betrayed you.

I could feel Shaarvan's eyes sweeping the field, still doing his duty as he spoke with me.

It was I who betrayed you, my love.

Shaarvan, I understand now why you left me. I am doing better about my projections, most of the time. You could help me to learn to stop them completely. I know you could. Please, let me come to Altar.

You are a temptress with your words, my love, but you would bring death to us all. One mistake, Shaara, and he would descend. Besides, I shall not have you endangered. Do you not understand that? How could I fight if I were worrying over your safety? Thenos has gone berserk. He would force you to be his queen. And he would hurt you, my love. Then he would kill our son. You must never come to Altar, not as long as Thenos lives. I command this. Promise me, Shaara.

I will obey you, my lord. I promise. But I do not understand. Why would Thenos . . .

I will not discuss Thenos with you, Shaara.

I could hear the sudden anger in his voice. I swallowed my questions. *I love you,* I told him.

He sighed, and I could feel the anger sliding from his thoughts.

You are the reason why I stay alive, my Shaara. Remember that, and remember that I shall come for you . . .

I had no tears left to cry that day. I rose up and went to Thandar, knowing that it was almost time for him to wake. I did not want to disturb Thal, who had come back in to join me and was sound asleep.

The babe suckled lustily, eager as always, my little bright-eyed wonder. I bent to kiss his head, and he stopped and stared at me. I stretched out my finger to him. He clasped it greedily. He plopped it into his mouth, but it had no milk. He let out a squeaky protest until I gave him my nipple again, and once more, he suckled greedily.

"You are so beautiful, my Thalia."

Thal made me jump. I turned and smiled at Thal. "I thought Shapechanger did not use meaningless words."

"Is that what Shaarvan told you?"

I nodded.

"It is true. The Shapechanger frown on *beautiful* especially. They prefer pleasing to the eye or intriguing, or perhaps poetic lines describing something wondrous, like the way your curls glow in the light from the moon with shadows and golden streaks that make me horny as heck."

I laughed. Thal could be so amusing.

"I think little Thandar is quite stuffed. He is enraptured with your face, too. Burp him and take him to his bed, my dear."

I obeyed. Thandar fussed a moment, but he was fed and warm and quickly went back to sleep.

When I returned to our bed, Thal's inviting arms were waiting for me. I settled into them.

"So you told Shaarvan about Tren?"

"How do you always know?"

"Usually there is a sadness in your eyes and a distance, although you attempt to pretend that there is not. Tonight, your manner is considerably lightened from your earlier gloom. I thank Shaarvan for his reassurance."

Thal's eyes narrowed as he stared at me. "But you are hiding something. Tell me, Thalia."

I sighed and looked down. "I can't. Please don't order me. It would hurt you."

Thal reached for my chin and brought up my eyes. "Untold truths wound more than falseness. Obey me, Wife."

I took in a long breath, but I didn't delay my compliance. Thal still held my chin. I couldn't hide from him.

"It is just that . . . I asked Shaarvan if I could go to Altar to be with him, and he said I'd bring death to them all."

"We knew that, Thalia. You broadcast."

"But — Shaarvan said that Thenos wanted to make me his queen. Why would Thenos do that? I am Shaarvan's wife. If Shaarvan did not Second Thenos to me, how could Thenos claim me?"

"So that is why Thenos searches for you . . ."

I ignored Thal's words and pursued my own question. Surely, Thal understood Shapechanger law better than I did. "But how could Thal claim me?"

"Power overrules all obstructions."

"But — I don't understand. Doesn't he still have to obey the laws? If I have a husband, how can Thenos claim me? Besides, Thenos is a Trendacons. He's my brother!"

"He has broken many laws, Thalia. He no longer follows the Shapechanger codes. You cannot expect him to do what is lawful or what is right. He is a meteor broken free from its orbit."

"He sure does enough damage to be a meteorite! I wish he would leave us all alone. I wish he would . . ."

"We will never let him have you, Thalia. Do not worry over it."

Stupidly, I started to cry again. I think it was from the hormones in my body and not from my fear of Thenos, but Thal's arms were comforting me, and his warm breath in my hair was sending delicious thoughts of desire throughout me.

Thal stopped as he read my thought and smiled at me. His lips touched mine with the briefest kiss, but I knew there would be no more. Thal's eyes were still questioning.

"It is curious that a trader would be fixated on one female when he could have any he chose. Does he love you, Thalia?"

"No!" I snapped out, repulsed by the idea.

I dropped my eyes so I would not see the warning in Thal's. I knew better than to raise my voice with a Shapechanger.

Thal didn't upbraid me for my failure, but he waited for a more suitable reply. I swallowed and attempted to explain. "Shaarvan told me once that Thenos always wanted most what he couldn't have. Maybe that's why Thenos thinks he wants me. I was the only one of Shaarvan's girls he couldn't steal."

Thal was silent a moment, looking at me. Then, he nodded as if he had made his own decision on the matter. "There is probably more to it than that, Thalia. You are very beautiful, and there is an essence of Power in you that tantalizes."

I smiled at Thal, but I shook my head. There were lots of girls more beautiful than me, and whatever Power I supposedly had, Thenos had always held so much more. Why would he desire mine?

"How often was Thenos near you?" Thal asked me, twirling my curls around his finger.

"Thenos used to come and play with Thaarac once or twice a week."

"And how were relations between you and Thenos?"

"We never even spoke. Shaarvan always guarded me. Thenos never did or said anything, except . . ."

"Yes? Tell me, Thalia."

Thal's fingers had stopped their play. His eyes were peering into mine with such intensity that I felt almost nervous. Why did it seem that my answer was so important to him?

"Thenos' eyes were always on me in an evil way, kind of lustful-like, and the way he stared at me made me cringe. And, it was the strangest thing, the last time I saw him, he spoke into my mind."

"What did he say, Thalia?"

"That's what's really odd. I can't remember; I only know that he spoke to me, and Shaarvan couldn't hear him."

"Did Thenos ever touch you, Shaara?"

"Yes. That last time. Shaarvan let him kiss my hand."

"Stars! That is it. That is when he did it. Did it hurt when he touched your hand?"

"Yes. Thenos' lips felt like the strap you used on me. They stung almost equally."

Thal nodded and rose up. "Thenos put some kind of bond on you, Shaara, right there in front of Shaarvan's eyes. I wonder how Shaarvan did not know."

Thaarac must have been having a bad dream. He cried out and then tossed his head. I watched as Thal got up and checked on him, pulling the blankets more firmly about him. He did the same for Thandar and then returned to the bed.

I continued. "After Shaarac's birth, when Thenos started coming to see Shaarac, Shaarvan never felt any of the evilness. It was weird because before that, Shaarvan had always mistrusted Thenos."

"Thenos learned many of the secrets of the Old Ones. But how could he bond you without a deeper touch? None of us could do that."

"Tren did."

"I can feel only a shadow of your bond with Tren. Shaarvan removed most of it."

"But Tren wasn't even Shapechanger, and he bonded me."

"A Shapechanger would never be disloyal to a female of the blood and place a bonding where none was permitted."

"Except Thenos?"

Thal snuggled me against him. "There is no question that Thenos is depraved, my dear. It is good that we had this talk. It is better to know one's enemy. But I shall not allow him to prey on your mind. You are far away from Thenos and will always remain so."

I would have continued my questions, but Thal pushed my head down onto his chest and said, "Forget Thenos. As I said, we shall not allow him to touch you again. And now that Tren is here, we have an entire army of Shapechangers to protect you."

"You'll accept Tren then?"

"Dawn approaches, my wife. Go to sleep."

Shaarvan

I am glad that Tren has followed Shaara to her mysterious planet. I think my wife has the need for a friend. Will Thal allow that friendship? Will the others welcome Tren to their midst? Tren will learn much if they give him half a chance. I am proud to claim him as my brother. He will do honor to the Trendacons.

Shaara has grown stronger in her Power if she can pull even a neophyte Shapechanger to her side. And the dreams we share across the stars are incredibly rare. Yet, I am not surprised; Shaara's transition brought the attention of the Old Ones. Even they discerned her specialness.

Oh, Shaara. I miss your smiles, your uplifted, stubborn chin, and the way you questioned me incessantly. I miss the joy you brought to me every day. I even miss your temper and your tears. Be safe, my love, be safe.

Tren

The Shapechanger males, who had used me as a punching bag earlier, were friendlier after we left the dwelling of Shaara and Thal. The bondmates took me to their living quarters. Thedar made up a bed for me and sat down to talk. He was much more affable than before. As we chatted, I decided I liked him.

Spelon was the one who bristled up every time he looked at me. I could feel his hatred. I wondered what I had done to get off on such bad footing. Surely, it was Thal whom I had offended, not Spelon.

However interesting Spelon's reaction was, I sensed the others were as angry with him as they had been with me. Neither Tenor nor Thedar answered when Spelon spoke. He growled at them a couple of times, and then, at last, he left us, pipe weapon in hand, tramping angrily out into the woods.

Tenor said he thought someone should go with him, but neither of them was enthusiastic about it. The subject kind of drifted off, and soon they were asking me about my training on Westla. I told them about spending time with the Old Ones and Tessa, and they laughed and chucked me on the back. Somehow, I think that I'd just joined their team.

Thalia

The next morning, Tren joined us for breakfast. His face was puffy and purplish in spots. I wanted to soothe the pain of it, but Thal's eyes watched me. He was not pleased with my thoughts.

Thal handed me a pillow for my sore bottom and then directed me to sit beside Spelon. I was still angry at the jerk, but of course, I didn't in any way reflect my feelings. I pushed the pillow under my bottom, sat rather hesitantly, and carefully kept my eyes lowered.

Tren and Thedar sat across from me. Thal sat on my other side, with our son beside him. For a moment, no one spoke as everyone reached for the hot, brewed drink in the mugs in front of us. One of the native trees was supplying the beverage. Its leaves, when dried, made a satisfactory brew, and we were all quite fond of it. In fact, Thal was concerned it might be slightly addictive, although he had found no harmful drugs in it.

Tenor had prepared the usual — cereal and the bread that I'd shown him how to bake — (Thal would still not allow me to cook.) Tenor had already eaten and left to do guard duty outside.

We were still drinking our first cup of coffee/tea when Thaarac began showing off. I think he was performing for the new Shapechanger who had come into our midst. Thaarac started reciting his newest learned verse of Shapechanger lore. You could barely understand what he was trying to say, but with his baby lisp, he was adorable. I smiled at him and wished he were sitting next to me so I could give him a big hug.

"Is that Shaarvan's son?" Tren asked, breaking up the warm feeling and our smiles.

There was silence and an indrawn breath all around. It was as if we all thought that Thal might fly into a sudden rage. Even Thaarac knew to be quiet.

But Thal did not erupt. He continued eating, and his eyes studied Tren thoughtfully. He glanced at me and then around the table before speaking.

"Thaarac is *my* son, Tren. More precise explanations would be better dealt with when the boy is outside."

I took a sip of my drink and nibbled nervously at my piece of bread. My bottom still smarted, and I wiggled to ease the pain. Spelon growled at me.

Tren, as if not sensing the tension in the room, blundered on. "When will Shaara be allowed to speak to me?"

"Thalia," Thedar reminded Tren.

Tren ignored it.

Once more, all eyes were looking at Thal. I dared take only a quick peek, and then I lowered my eyes, feeling it was safer to do so. I was starting to feel nauseous from all the tension. I placed my piece of bread back on the plate and took another sip of the tea.

Thedar poured himself more. He offered me some, but I shook my head. My cup was still full.

"You have not eaten a sufficient quantity, Thalia," Spelon said, picking up my bread and handing it back to me. "You must eat heartily to feed our newest baby Warlord."

I felt like sticking my tongue out at him, but Thal was watching me too carefully to allow me even a glare at Spelon. I took the bread from the jerk and bit into it.

Tren's question had still gone unanswered. Thal spooned in some cereal. He didn't look eager to discuss it or anything else at breakfast.

"I am confused, Thal," Tren said with a conniving look on his face. "I thought you told me yesterday that you were Thalia's husband, yet today Spelon seems to be . . ."

"Enough," Thal ordered abruptly. "We shall not allow you to sow discord among us."

"Well done," Thedar said as he filled his bowl with more cereal and then passed the serving dish to Spelon.

Tren had the good sense to stop pressing. He looked around the table, raised his hands, and gave the male sign that acknowledged that the error was his.

Thal studied Tren for a moment and then nodded, satisfied that Tren had backed down. "Spelon is Thalia's Second. He governs her, as do I and the others."

"I thought you were the Second . . . " Tren interrupted. The puzzlement on his face gave proof of the sincerity of his confusion. None of the males had the heart to remind Tren of his second blunder.

Thaarac began banging his wooden utensil against his bowl. Thal's eyes moved down to meet his wiggly son's. He smiled at him and said, "Thaarac, if you are finished, you may go outside and join Tenor."

Our son sprang out of his chair, dropped a kiss on my arm, which was as high as he could reach, and said, "Bye-bye, Mommy," before I could grab him and kiss him properly. Thaarac skipped out the door.

Thal waited a moment for the door to close and then turned back to Tren. "There are many things a Shapechanger male does not discuss when a woman is present. Although your training has obviously been short, I am sure that you are aware of that. When you have learned to examine a new environment in the manner of a Shapechanger, absorbing knowledge from the air and the currents around you, you will no longer find the need for so many inquiries."

"Yeah, you ask as many questions as a female," Spelon said, sneering at Tren and then at me.

I could see that Tren did not appreciate the males' rebukes, but he didn't react to them. "You are right. My training to be a Shapechanger was short. I have been impatient to locate Shaara and offer my services."

"Thalia," Thal reminded him.

"I cannot yet take in information from the air like the rest of you," Tren sighed impatiently. "I repeat — when will Thalia be allowed to speak with me?"

"Never," Spelon said. "She can answer a direct question that you pose to her, but she cannot talk freely with you. Your level is not high enough."

"Spelon, that's not fair!" I said with a bit more anger in my voice than I should have used.

"Do you wish to be sent to your room?" Thal warned.

"She has still not eaten. Her cereal is untouched," Spelon reminded Thal.

I shook my head and picked up the hollow wooden utensil that we used for cereal. As the four males watched, I took my first bite. It was cold and bland as a paste.

Thal turned back to Tren. "Thalia may only speak freely with the Shapechanger Lords of her bonding."

"She and I are bonded. But what is this lord business? I thought all Shapechangers were lords," Tren said.

Spelon laughed at Tren's ignorance. I wished I could give the jerk a sharp kick under the table. I took another bite of cereal to avoid Thal's flashing eyes.

Thal poured more tea for me and for himself and then passed the pot to Tren before continuing with his lecture. "On Freinana and many of the outer planets, all Shapechangers are addressed as *lords*, but the true *Lords* are only the highest of the families of Westla. Those families have a lineage that can be traced directly back to the Old Ones. Each of these descendants is brought to Westla for testing, and those who score with a high level of intelligence, superior force, and Power are given the special name of *Warlord*. We bondmates are all of this high rank of *Warlords*. What did your tests show? What is your placement?"

Once more, Spelon snickered, "Tren is barely Shapechanger, Thal. He is a changeover. Why would they bother to test him?"

I raised my eyes and glared at Spelon. Thedar, sitting next to me on my other side, patted my hand and asked, "Thalia, how is little Thandar today?"

Everyone stared at me. "He is well. He is sleeping now," I answered and then dropped my eyes. I knew that Thedar had been trying to warn me about my anger.

Tren was not entirely insensitive to the currents flowing around him. He stared at Thedar a moment and at the hand that had touched mine. His eyebrow raised, and he looked pointedly at Thal.

"You allow the others much freedom with her," Tren said.

Thal shrugged. "Thalia knows she is mine. At times, it takes all of us to watch over her and Thaarac — and now little Thandar."

"Shaarvan would not have allowed it."

Thal sipped his drink calmly and eyed Tren. "You have much to learn about the Shapechanger. I told you last night, it was Shaarvan that forged this link."

"So you say," Tren said, ignoring Spelon's growl.

Thal ignored both of them and continued. "In spite of your troublesome questions, I have decided that I shall permit you to join our group . . ."

"We do not need him," Spelon interrupted.

"He was sent by Westla," Thedar reminded Spelon.

Thal held up his hand to continue. "As I said, Tren, you will be allowed to join us. However, we must see that your ship is well camouflaged. Thedar, would you and Tenor accompany Tren back to his ship and make sure of it?"

Thedar nodded. I sighed in relief and looked up. Spelon started once again to badger me about not eating, but Thal, bless his soul, waved him silent.

"What good is Tren to us?" Spelon demanded. "Why should we let him stay?"

"You forget, Spelon. It is safer for Thalia if Tren does not depart. In fact, we would have to kill Tren if he attempted to leave the planet," Thal said, meeting Tren's eyes.

"No!" I cried out. "How could you even think about . . . ?"

Spelon had moved behind me to drape his hand on my shoulder. Angrily, I pushed it off. I hadn't needed his reminder. Thal's eyes had already indicated I'd displeased him. My rough treatment of Spelon's caution brought on a flash of Thal's hand. I'd just received First Warning.

Tren was, of course, watching everything as if he were videorecording it. It was embarrassing that he'd been the witness of my disgrace.

"Spelon, sit down," Thal ordered.

I breathed a sigh of relief. I was far less likely to get in trouble with Spelon not hovering above me. He pulled out a chair and sat next to me. I looked over at Thal to see how angry he was.

He flashed Second Warning.

"Do not worry, Thalia. They would have to kill me to force me away from you," Tren said.

"Why is that?" Thal asked, turning back to regard Tren.

"Thalia does not need your assistance. She is already well-guarded," Spelon interjected.

Thal and Tren both ignored him.

"Tessa told me that Shaara will need me," Tren said.

"Tessa?" Thal turned his full attention on Tren. "Tessa spoke with you? Why would she take an interest in a changeover?"

"Who would want her to take an interest? That old witch," Spelon said.

Again, Tren ignored Spelon and answered Tren. "I was instructed by the Old Ones. Tessa was often at my side."

"Interesting. I asked you once, but you did not have the opportunity to answer. Did they test you?"

"I was never tested," Tren admitted. "There was no time."

Spelon laughed. He picked up a berry from his plate and tried to plop it into my mouth. "I told you," Spelon said, not looking up but instead concentrating on me. "Why would they waste energy on a changeover?"

"Thalia."

I wasn't hungry anymore. The conversation had completely taken my hunger away, but Second Warning didn't allow for argument. I opened my mouth and accepted the berry.

"So you are unranked as we had assumed," Thal continued. "Sadly, Spelon is correct. You will not be permitted to speak with Thalia, and except for meals, you must stay away from her. She is ranked far above you."

"Above me?" Tren said, looking me over like I had a say in the matter. "Wait a minute, Thal. Because I wasn't — was not tested, you are going to keep me away from Thalia?"

"What did you expect?" Spelon laughed, still ridiculing Tren.

I almost glared at Spelon, but I caught myself in time.

"Shaarvan's wife is a Trendacons, the uppermost rank of Altar and Westla. As you probably know, Shaarvan's uncle is the Highest. Shaarvan will probably be next in line for the position."

"Yes, I know, Tem. He and I talked often."

Thal raised his eyebrow at that. I could tell he doubted how chummy Tren and Tem were.

"Thalia received the DNA of the Trendacons, so her station is of equal rank with Shaarvan and his uncle," Thal explained to Tren and then motioned for Spelon to stop sticking berries into my mouth. "It is, therefore, unreasonable for you to expect . . ."

"Good," Tren said, looking extremely pleased with himself. "Then we have no problem. Shaarvan made me his brother. I am a Trendacons as well."

I gasped and started to cough. I had forgotten. In the casino, when Tren had refused to allow me to drink whatever it was called, and Shaarvan had done something horrible to the slaver, Shaarvan had given Tren Thenos' place in the family. I remembered it now.

Spelon shoved my mug in my face. I would have argued about that, but I needed the drink.

"Thalia, is that true?" Thal demanded.

I nodded.

Thal studied me a moment, and then he smiled. "Well, then the discussion is at an end. Welcome to our group, Tren. Since you are Thalia's brother, I shall allow my wife to speak freely with you, but . . ." Thal looked from Tren to me and back again. His eyes grew dark with warning. "But brothers and sisters do not kiss, nor, Thalia, shall I allow you to touch Tren or he to touch you."

"You trust what a changeover says?" Spelon said, spitting his drink back into the cup.

"Do you accuse my wife of lying?" Thal asked. The pattern of his Change showed its shadow. I shuddered, not out of fear but because such a challenge usually ended in violence.

"No, of course not," Spelon burst out, chagrined by his mistake. "Forgive me."

I smiled at Tren. Everything was going to be all right. I was so happy I couldn't help bursting out with the one thing that had really bothered me. "I never called you, Tren. I've never called anyone to me. I don't even know how."

"Thalia!" Thal roared.

I suddenly remembered I was in Second Warning. I dropped my eyes and flashed an apology.

"Do you accept these conditions, Tren?" Thal asked.

"Yes."

"My wife, at times, forgets to modulate her voice," Thal said, looking more at me than at Tren. "I am sure she did not realize that what we have just learned makes you a Shapechanger Lord."

"Of course," Tren said, and I think he was laughing at me, but I didn't dare look up to see.

"Have you forgotten the rules we *discussed* yesterday, Thalia?" Thal demanded sharply.

"No, my Lord." I stared into Thal's eyes. Of course, I remembered the pain he had given me. I was still very careful about how I wiggled, even on the pillow.

"The same rules apply to your brother, Thalia."

I lowered my eyes in obedience. "I will obey," I said.

Tren stared at us a moment and then whistled. "Targone told me, but I never thought I would see it. How the high and mighty have fallen."

Tren's words stung. They made my tears start. I kept my eyes down away from his regard and asked Thal if I could leave to go feed Thandar.

Thal nodded, and I got up and walked away.

Why had Tren been so cruel? I paced back and forth and tried out the words I wished I could have said. Tren had been unfair. Didn't he realize that I didn't have a choice about my obedience? Hadn't he seen enough of the Power of the Shapechanger to understand that I couldn't fight it? Or had transition brought him to the level of the very young, when they were caustic as lye to every girl?

Thenos

She is out there. I can feel it. But what planet is she on? Where must I send Chaslow? The trail is cold, and I have not been able to link up with Thenosa again. I thought about ordering Chaslow back to

Westla, but Thenosa's bondmates would not be foolish enough to return her there. They must have taken her farther away. But where?

I have ordered my researchers to pore through the data on safe-zone planets. One of them must harbor my princess. I ordered them to exclude planets with harsh conditions or dangerous predators. Her bondmates would never endanger her. How many planets can there be which would be suitable? It does not matter. I shall find her.

In the meantime, my new palace is finished. I am quite pleased with it. I have had it built in the city of Altar, close to the Judgment Chambers. My princess will be quite comfortable in her new dwelling.

I have successfully concluded several other matters of business as well. Shaarvan was declared officially dead, and I have been formally wedded to my beautiful young bride. An old-fashioned street shuttle, decorated in flowers and vines, wound through the streets, and the peasants, believing us to be in it, chanted their greetings.

"Princess Thenosa," they shouted as the guards flung copper coins into their midst. I had special foods distributed throughout the city so they could share in my happiness. They will not forget. Already, the people love you, my princess.

I prepared death documents next. Of course, I shall not need them, but the Commoner's Senate that I have caused to be created requested them. Amazingly, it provided me with considerable pleasure to gratify their wishes. Does not everyone find contentment in the perpetuation of a legacy?

I have named Princess Thenosa my queen and have given her the reign of the planet Altar at my Passing. Poor little captive, so frightened, so naive — how fitting it would be to see the future of my kingdom in her hands. I shall give her such power, my little one. Will she savor it appropriately? What a pity that I would not be there to see her rule. Even in my death, she would have no choice but to praise my name and remember me with the kindest thoughts.

My Death Documents have proclaimed Thenosa my heir. Prince Thenon will rule after my beloved. Of course, my son will one day sit on my throne. Why have I worked so hard, if not to ensure that my name will live forever? Destiny tells me that my name will be etched in Altar's history. This palace and my dynasty will stand forever.

The Commoner's Senate has taken all these documents to Curtroon for safekeeping, where I have established a fortress as a backup to my plans. The Curtroon guards will protect the documents.

In Curtroon, I have even established a Queen's guard. They are in training now for the day when Thenosa arrives. My princess must always be guarded. I shall never grant her the freedom to roam unattended.

But, of course, I shall not die anytime soon. I am healthy. The drugs have fortified me so that I may live hundreds of years longer than others. I suppose it is possible that Thenosa might die before me. I cannot have that. Perhaps I shall inject her with drugs.

But I shall not worry about that now, only that I am ready for her arrival. I am sure my preparations will please her.

Senuck and Nedrof, two nearby cities, I have made training grounds for my troops. Shaarvan and his followers think my defenses are dying. They will grow careless soon, and their mind force will wither like an ill-watered plant. Then, I shall conquer with an army of men. Shapechanger will learn that Power is not everything. There is victory in numbers!

It will all fit admirably. I am King, sometimes Emperor — perhaps both. King of Altar, Emperor of Westla, and the other planets under my "guidance." Yes. That is appropriate. From my throne, beside the seat of my adored Queen, I can almost see the pieces flying through the air and reassembling before me. It is good to be me. See what I have accomplished. See the worlds that I shall fashion into my liking?

Thalia

I am sure it was difficult for Tren to fit in at first. I hope it was. Since he arrived, his comments to me have all been cruel jabs. He is constantly ridiculing my new meek manner and seems to enjoy reminding me of how I used to be the once audacious little landoor groom.

Spelon seems to enjoy Tren's scorn. The two of them have formed a friendship. I can just imagine them sitting around, poking fun at me.

I have been able to maintain my calm with Tren and Spelon's taunts about my submission, but when Tren attacks me for betraying Shaarvan, I can never stop my tears. He and Spelon deserve each other. I am beginning to hate them both.

To Tenor and Thedar, I am as sweet as I can be — even more so than usual — but to Tren and Spelon, I am polite, obedient, and glacial.

A twentyTide has passed, a twentyTide of boredom. Spelon no longer takes me for walks, and Thal does not allow me to work in the garden or bake bread, nor am I permitted even the smallest chore. He expects me to rest and watch everyone else do all the work. I feel like screaming at the monotony of it.

Then, this morning, Thal declared a holiday! He says that at the edge of morning, we shall all go celebrate Tren's arrival and Thandar's birth. I am so elated. Tenor and I have gotten together and thought up all kinds of delicious things to eat, and Thal has relented enough to let me help prepare them. I can't wait!

Tren

I have taken Thal's advice and am attempting to let the currents in the air teach me of the moods and feelings of those around me, but I am bombarded with too many stimuli. It all confuses me. How does the Shapechanger sort through it?

Spelon's gruffness covers the softest heart. He is a giant of a tree, yet his fingers treat a wounded Stubra as if it were a baby. He is the easiest on my mind. His thoughts are the most clear and unblended. He and I have become friends.

Thedar, a gentle and older male, has iron in his veins. He is not so easy to read. Yet, I think I am becoming more perceptive of his moods and reasonings. Tenor, likewise, is more clear-cut, although he has a depth that I despair of entering. Neither of them has been overly friendly. They seem irritated by me for some reason.

Thal . . . I cannot begin to understand him. He hides from me, and his thoughts are like the flashes of light in the night sky. Their effect is almost nullifying my deliberations, and the after-image is gone before I can judge the light's direction or the color of his thoughts. I fear that it will be many sevenTides before I can feel comfortable with him.

And Thalia — she is the worst. To be around her is to be assaulted by twenty horns, all playing different notes. She throws off surges of emotions that differ with each second's passing. It is an ache of discord. I focus on the strongest forces and find that she is full of apprehension and fear. My muscles gather to step forward and fight, not knowing where to face the enemy when I am suddenly dashed with a spray of anger and rebellion.

I gather up the words to slay her insurgence and at once am stricken with her humbleness, and I see her downcast eyes and lowered head. I attempt to study her face to make sure that I am reading her, and then I am even more confused by it. Her face conflicts with every emotion I feel pouring from her soul.

I have spoken with Spelon concerning it. He laughs and tells me that all of them have to continuously fortify their shields against her emotional assaults. "No one can follow a female of such contradictions. To stay in tune with her is like sky surfing on the ups and downs of the air currents. She is a warrior and yet not a warrior.

"She is a child, no more mature than Shaarac, and yet a full-blooded woman who has born two sons. She is a sage who is still driven by pure emotion. There is no arranging her into suitable categories, She is Thalia — a unique." Spelon said with a hint of vexation but also with a kernel of respect. When his outpouring was concluded, he shook his head, grunted, and then flashed a gesture that I think meant *ignore my words*. I had often seen it used among drunkards.

I could see that his analysis caused him some dishevel. She was probably a cancer to his complacency. I had to agree with his conclusion to some degree. Shaara, or Thalia as they called her here, was an enigma in all versions. It was better that I keep away if I could only convince myself to do so. But she harbored a magnetic force that held me to her. Even when I turned away, my feet walked me back to her.

If only I were Shaarvan. Then I could read her, force my way inside her soul, and understand her. I would not dare to try that yet. I might hurt her with my inexperience. But I could see that I was injuring her every day with my awkwardness and my inability to block her out. I did not know what to do or how to stop.

As a commoner, I had always confronted problems head-on. I was Shapechanger now, but that philosophy had not been altered within me. At last, I sought out Thal to ask for help. It was especially hard for me to do so since I barely trusted him, yet Thedar and Tenor had both rebuffed me when I'd asked them.

I knew what asking Thal would entail. I must accept that Thal was Thalia's husband. That was the first step and the hardest. Would he be willing to offer me assistance? I could no longer keep bringing tears to Thalia's eyes. Why would I want to torment the one I adored? Yet, did I dare admit that to Thal? Would he kill me if I did so?

Thalia

The time arrived for our party, and we walked together to the creek where Thal and I had pretended the mermaid scene. He and I smiled over the memories. Tren intercepted the look. I felt his quick flash of anger. It brought tears to my eyes. I shrugged it off, pretending I hadn't noticed.

I worked extra hard that morning at being sweet with Tenor and Thedar. I wanted to emphasize how much I favored them while making sure, of course, that Thal was always the one who received the biggest share of my smiles and thoughtfulness. I did my best to completely ignore Spelon and Tren.

Thandar was a doll. He was content to lie in my lap and gurgle his happiness, but Thaarac scrambled up and about. He was too active for me to do more than watch and try to keep him in sight. I didn't worry much. The bondmates never allowed him to get into mischief. How many mothers are so fortunate to have such ready and eager babysitters?

I was happy as a bubbling brook to be out and away from the house. Because of that, it took me almost until the sun's zenith before I realized that Thal was not pleased with me. He had said nothing, but I could tell. All my smiles and touches on his arm had not brought me a single smile from him, nor one loving look since that first shared memory of Mermaid Creek.

I felt like crying when I realized it. I could not stand having Thal disappointed in me. What had I done? I searched my mind for faults in my behavior.

At last, when the others had slipped away and we were alone, Thal ordered me to sit beside him. Thedar was watching Thandar. He had rocked the baby to sleep. Thandar was happily making his little suckling noises and snoring softly. Thaarac was likewise entertained and safe with Tenor. I snuggled down beside Thal and gave him all my attention.

He took my hand in his. His was rough from gardening, but I enjoyed the feel of it. I clutched at its great size and waited for his words.

"Thalia, I have seen a woman break up an army of men."

He had my attention wholeheartedly. I stopped worrying about his unhappiness with me. My mind flitted about, trying to imagine how I could possibly be helpful to Shaarvan.

"No, Thalia, this is not about Shaarvan. It is about you."

I breathed in sharply and held my breath. Thal was going to tell me something awful. I knew it, yet I couldn't wait for him to explain. I wished desperately that I dared probe his thoughts.

"The woman I am speaking of, Thalia, broke the army up by flirting, withdrawing, picking favorites, and changing her mind again and again. It is an ugly woman who tramples men's hearts like that. It always destroys the unity of the whole."

Thal stood up then and looked down at me. "You are an intelligent woman, Thalia. Think about it."

I didn't want Thal to leave. I clung to his hand and begged him not to walk away. I had started to cry, but he ignored it. Gently, he disentangled me, ordered me to stay, and then moved away as if he could not bear to stay in my company.

I adjusted myself on the grassy spot I was sitting on and thought about Shaarvan and Thenos. Did Thal mean that I had somehow caused all the problems between them? I wasn't Helen of Troy, I knew I couldn't cause a war, and Teea, Shaarvan's mother, had told me I wasn't responsible for the gulf between the brothers.

But Thal had said this was not about Shaarvan. I sighed and wept briefly and continued to think about Thal's words.

It took me a long time before I realized that Thal had been talking about our little group. When I looked at what I had done, I saw the discord. Spelon was alone, no longer friends with Tenor and Thedar. Tren was off by himself, sulking, no doubt. Thedar and Tenor had not reacted well to my pleasantries, as if even they no longer wanted to associate with me.

I understood then what Thal wanted me to see. I had been a fool. My disposition had been a rotten fruit in a bowl full of good ones. The nastiness of my contagion would soon spread to the others, forcing an entire bowl of fruit to be cast out. No wonder Thal had walked away from me. I would leave me, too, if I could.

I had made others suffer just because I'd gotten into trouble. Tren had traveled for a manyTide because he thought I needed him. Then, he kept hurting me because he didn't understand, and because of that, I'd launched so spiteful an attack that Tren was probably wondering why he'd ever come looking for me.

Spelon, abrasive as he was, had given up his whole life on Westla just to protect me, and I'd returned his service with childish rebellions and disobedience.

Had I been mean to Thedar and Tenor, too? Had I embroiled them in my war games, making them choose sides, making them alienate Spelon and Tren, breaking apart the unity of the whole, as Thal had said?

No wonder Thal was disappointed in me. I had been a brat and a user, a selfish woman who had thought only of her own desires. I didn't deserve his goodness. I didn't deserve any of them!

Thal —who had given me everything — how had I repaid him? I had been difficult, unloving, and the cause of all of his problems. He'd had to leave his telescope and all his fine studies and live on a primitive planet just so he could keep me safe. And he'd never complained about it. He was always kind to me, yet I caused nonstop problems . . .

I'd long ago stopped wondering why Shaarvan had chosen Thal to be my husband. Thedar had warned me that Shaarvan never did things without a purpose. I'd watched Shaarvan play the game ranex, a game similar to chess where the moves had to be planned logically for turns to come. Shaarvan had always won. His mind was like that: weaving and interweaving probabilities, shifting directions, and refiguring the odds. Even Tren had said that Shaarvan was the one person he would not gamble against.

And Shaarvan had chosen Thal because he knew I'd admire him. Shaarvan had known I could learn from my Second. What had Shaarvan wanted me to learn?

I knew a woman on Terra who was delving deeply into metaphysics. She'd told me that we draw into our lives what we most need to learn. What if Shaarvan were still far away from me because I hadn't taken the time to learn whatever I needed to learn? What if the Fates would not allow Shaarvan to return to me until I'd figured it all out?

I went to Thal and sat down beside him. Thaarac also lay there, but my son was sound asleep, tired out from his play. What precious morsels had my firstborn swallowed that I'd missed by dallying in my silly dramas?

"I am sorry, Thal," I said. "I understand what you wanted me to see. I have been a selfish and childish fool. I will never divide the unity of the group again. I promise you.

"And I understand more. Shaarvan wanted me to learn from you, didn't he? He wanted you to teach me, and I never even thought about it. What did Shaarvan want me to learn? Please, Thal, please tell me. Will you teach me? I will try hard to learn. I will be your best student."

There was a hint of a smile in the corner of Thal's lips and in his eyes. "Shaarvan told me you would say that to me one day, Thalia. I had begun to doubt."

"I know. I've been blind to Shaarvan's wishes, haven't I? I should have examined things more carefully. I've been so stupid. All I could think about was what I wanted. I never thought about . . . " I shook my head. "It was Shaarvan who sent Tren here. He wanted me to learn from all of you, and I've wasted so much time."

"Time is never wasted, Thalia. You have learned a great many other things. Shaarvan knew your Power would be great, but you have soared to amazing heights. He could not have envisioned that for you."

"I've only tested to Level Four. Why do you always say my level is rising?"

"You carry whole conversations with Shaarvan across a galaxy. Does that not surprise you?"

"That's Shaarvan."

"Shaarvan and you. Together, you hold open a link whose scope I have never heard of. You called Tren here, Thalia. Shaarvan could not have done so. He does not know where we are."

"I don't either. And I never even thought about Tren . . ."

"You impress me, Thalia. Were you not as humble as you are, I would teach you nothing. But there is no arrogance in you. Nor does your Power seem to make you more rebellious. I shall be delighted to teach you."

I made my peace with Spelon and Tren, then. I apologized for my pettiness. Neither one of them showed it on their faces, but I could read the relief in their hearts. I felt enormous guilt for the grief I'd caused them.

Tren wasn't ready to let his anger go yet. I felt it in him, but there was nothing more I could do for him.

We ate our lunch and relaxed for a while. Already, I could feel the difference among my bondmates. How could I have been so blind to the discontent of the group? How could I have ignored it?

In the late afternoon, we went swimming in a place where the water deepened into a pool. Thaarac had never swum before, and he splashed around and laughed a great deal. He got Spelon and Thedar wet before they had the chance to disrobe. Thal told the rest of us to strip so we would have dry clothes on the way back. I thought he meant everybody but me. When he turned that look on me, I paled.

"All right, everyone, turn and face the other way. My wife is shy," Thal said, laughing gently.

Obediently, everyone turned.

"I have to hold Thandar," I told my husband.

He took Thandar from me and ordered me to shed my dress. I was fast. I ran into the water before Thal could tell everyone to turn back around.

So I was stuck in the deep part of the pool. Thal laughed at that. He made Tren babysit the baby and dove in. The water was lovely, and for twenty minutes, I was completely happy, but then my teeth started to chatter, and I wanted out. Tren laughed, but Thal made everyone turn around again.

My dress stuck to my back since I was in such a hurry to be clothed. Thal's arms went around me, and he worked on warming me. Then Tren brought Thandar over to us.

But even after I took back the baby, Tren stood there staring at me strangely. "Who beat you, Thalia, and why?" he demanded.

"I did," Thal told him. "She was beaten because she was rude to a Shapechanger. Of course, she was trying to save your life at the time."

I could feel everyone's eyes on us. Even Thaarac was listening. I blushed and hung my head.

"I am sorry. I did not mean for my arrival to bring you pain," Tren said stiffly.

"There were other lessons she learned in her punishment," Thal told him. Thal's arm dropped over me and pulled me tightly against his body in the Shapechanger hold.

Thal began testing Tren. His hand dropped down to fondle my breast. I froze, not daring to breathe. I didn't look up at the others, but I could feel them watching. If Tren mentioned Thal's treatment of me, things could get a hundred times worse. I knew not to react. I hoped Tren did, too.

Apparently, Tren knew enough to ignore Thal's fondling of me. He continued as if he were merely making conversation. "I am new to the Shapechanger, Thal, and I appreciate your understanding of my ignorance in many matters, but I have one last question," Tren said, "and I would like Thalia to answer it."

Tren's eyes had grown hard. I could feel his anger. Didn't he know that the others could feel it, too?

"Thalia has permission to respond to your question," Thal told him easily, but the hand on my breast had not stilled.

"Thalia, my question is this. Did you go willingly to Thal's bed that first time?"

I gasped at Tren's cruelty. I drew in a sharp breath and held it, determined not to cry.

Thal's hand stilled. He raised it to my shoulder and kissed my cheek. I couldn't look at Tren. I stared down at the grass between my naked feet.

Thal's eyes watched me as the silence continued. After a moment, he spoke. "Thalia chooses not to answer you, Tren, but I know you will plague her to tears with it, so I shall tell you what you want to know. The day I first took Thalia, she fought me like a wild cat. I had to beat her for it, and the taking of her used every trick I knew as a Shapechanger. It was still as close to rape as I have ever gone. She was webbed as securely as if I had tied her to the bed.

"And, after that, she almost killed herself. Her Power is strong enough for her to find the Path of Passing. Did you know that, Tren? To keep Thalia alive, I had to impregnate her. It was only the seeding of Thandar that finally forced Thalia's body to accept me."

Thal turned me to face him, and he laid my head on his chest. "Shaarvan has ordered her to obey me, Tren. I told you that, but I did not make it clear that she still talks with him every night. They have a mind link clear across the stars. And even though Thalia has given me this son, I have no illusions about her loyalty to Shaarvan. Her soulmate is on Altar."

Thal was holding me too tightly for me to kiss his face, but he knew my thought. His lips kissed the top of my head before he continued. "I know you are hurting Thalia because you love her and cannot have her. Look around. We all love her, Tren, and none of us will ever truly own her."

"He is right, Tren," Tenor said, and I heard Spelon and Thedar all agree.

I was crying again. How did my body keep finding so many tears? Pressed against Thal's chest, I felt his shirt growing wetter.

"Anything else you would like to know before you give Thalia peace?" Thal asked.

"What do you mean — she talks to Shaarvan across the stars? How is that possible?"

"At first, she did it in her dreams. Then, somehow, they forged a link, and now they talk through space. I do not know how they do it, but they do."

"Thalia, does Shaarvan know I am here?" Tren asked.

I nodded.

"Does he know where you are?" Thedar asked.

"No. I don't know where I am," I answered him.

"How is the war going?" Tenor asked.

"Shaarvan won't tell me. He refuses to discuss it."

Spelon came closer and placed his hand on my back. "I have an apology to make to you. I did not know how it was between you and Shaarvan. I did not understand about the link. Forgive me, Thalia."

What could I say? I'd deserved what he'd caused to happen.

"I thought things were different," Spelon continued.

"Thal is a good husband. I'm unfair to him. I wish I were otherwise," I said.

Tren moved closer. "I, too, apologize. I have whipped you with my words more cruelly than the strap that branded your skin. I have only wished for your happiness, Thalia. I cannot understand my abuse of you."

Thal loosened his hold. I swung around to look at my bondmates. "None of you understand. There is love between Thal and me. I know it is wrong, but I'm eager for Thal's touch, and even though I betray Shaarvan in this, I cannot fight it."

Thal took my hand and kissed it. "You do not betray your Shaarvan, Thalia. I have told you this. Shaarvan ordered you to my arms. It is the bonding and the training that now make you crave my touch. If Shaarvan should land on this planet and take one step towards you, no overlay of bonding would hold you to me. There is no disloyalty in you, Thalia."

I was glad Thandar began to fuss then, displaying his hunger. My eyes were flowing with tears. I wondered why rivers in their eyes, didn't bother men.

The baby nuzzled at my breast, but it was covered, milk unattainable. Thandar howled with the injustice of it. Thal led me away from the other Shapechanger males and helped me to sit down on a grassy knoll. He spread his legs around my bottom and leaned me back against him. His arms held his son's head while Thandar drank the warm, rich milk.

Then Thal whispered in my ear, "It is better to weep a river, Thalia, as women do. Men may only carry the sadness with them until they are able to fight some imagined foe and work it out. Think how difficult it would be to nurse your son while fighting. Surely, harboring the distress inside you would make the milk taste of sadness. It is much better your way."

I tried to kiss Thal with my lips, but I couldn't reach him.

"Stop that, woman," he told me playfully. "I have grown a bone in my thighs that has no place to go. Have compassion for me."

I laughed, but there was a ring of truth in his tale, and I remembered how difficult Shaarvan had found his abstinence.

Later, when I thought about it, I couldn't help my curiosity. "Thal, if it causes pain in Shapechanger men to wait for the end of abstinence, how can my three bondmates and Tren survive their unending drought?"

Thal laughed and tossed a clod of dirt. "Thalia," he said, "that part of the curriculum is not assigned. Leave off and think of other things."

That night, I asked my other husband.

"Shaarvan?"

"Question time?"

"What do you do about sex?"

"My blushing bride using words like that."

I knew he mocked me. I could almost see his eyes flashing with laughter. *"So your curiosity is still alive and well. What did Thal say?"*

"That it was not part of my curriculum."

Shaarvan laughed again. Even across space, I could picture his dimples. A sharp pang of desire spread through my limbs.

"I love you, Shaara, but there are things you do not need to know," he said.

"Why?"

"Do you know how frustrating it is not to kiss you silent? I love you, my . . . "

There was a chuckling under the covers. I heard it again. "Thal? You are awake?"

"How could I not be? Your frustration resounded off the mountains!"

"I'm sorry I woke you."

"He would not answer you, either, huh?"

"How did you know what we talked about?"

"Thalia, you are as predictable as the rotation of the planets."

"I thought you said I was unpredictable."

"No, I said, *not logical.* There is a difference."

It was later in the night that I saw Thenos. He looked like Shaarvan, but he was not.

"Come to me," he called. *"Come!"*

"No!" I yelled, and I woke up sobbing. Thal's arms were there, warm and gentle, but I continued to shiver.

"What is wrong? Tell me," he ordered.

"It was Thenos. He commanded me to come to him."

"Stars!"

Thal was up and dressing immediately. "Thalia, dress. I shall call the others."

"Maybe it was just a dream," I called after him.

"No argument. Up!"

Thal gathered everyone in the kitchen and began pacing back and forth like a general ordering the division of labor of his troops.

"Thenos has found her."

Everyone turned to stare at me.

"We will have to go further away. We must move beyond his abilities."

"Thal," I said, "I did not tell him where we are."

"You don't have to tell him anything. You are open."

"But I don't know where we are!"

"Thankfully," said Tenor.

"Contact Shaarvan, Thalia. Tell him we have to move out of range."

"What do you mean — out of range? You mean where I can't talk to Shaarvan anymore?"

"Do it now, Thalia. Tell him of Thenos."

I closed my eyes and tried to reach Shaarvan. He was sleeping, but he woke with the feel of me.

"*My love, how pleasant to feel you in my bed.*"

"Shaarvan," I sobbed. *"Thal commanded me to tell you that Thenos woke me up and ordered me to come to him."*

"Stars in Heaven! How has he gotten so much Power? Tell Thal to take you farther. You may not talk with me again, Shaara. It endangers you. Tell Thal to give you Shawl now. Obey me, Shaara. I love you forever and ever, and I shall find you — my soul, my body, my heart. Obey."

He severed the contact, and I fell apart.

"Tell me everything he said, Thalia. Now!" Thal ordered.

"Shaarvan said we must go farther away. He said I couldn't talk with him anymore." I started crying harder.

"Stop it! Thalia." Thal began to shake me, but I only blubbered worse.

Thedar laid his hand on Thal. "Let me talk to her."

Thedar tried to take me away from Thal, but I didn't want to go with him. I fought his arms. Only when Thal commanded it did I allow Thedar to lead me away to the other side of the room.

"Listen to me, Thalia. Your sons need you. Listen to my voice. Thaarac is in danger."

"What?"

"You heard me. Thaarac is in danger. Thenos will hurt him. You must tell me everything Shaarvan said. It is important for Thaarac."

"Don't let him hurt Thaarac. Please."

"Easy, Thalia. Listen to me. You must tell me what Shaarvan said. Tell me, Thalia."

"He said to go far away and not to talk to him anymore."

"Anything else, Thalia?"

"To take a shawl. But I don't have a shawl."

Tren sprang up. "Shawl, it is a drug that will put her to sleep. I have some. Sometimes we used it with girls who . . . I shall get it."

I fed Thandar, and then we started walking. Spelon and Thal took turns carrying me. They said I walked too slowly. I don't remember much of the trip, but at some point when we were still in the forest, Tren injected me with something. Everything was hazy after that.

They woke me to feed Thandar, and then each time I finished, Tren gave me another shot, and I was sent back to sleep. I remember waking up once and being surprised because I was on the ship already. I think I remember asking Thal if the drug would harm Thandar, and he told me *no*, but maybe that was a dream. I had so many dreams during that time.

We traveled for four days before I was allowed to awaken fully. Thal was bathing my face with water when I opened my eyes.

"We are approaching Sistema, Thalia. Tren will sell his ship there," Thal told me, and he left me to get dressed.

The drugged sleep had left me ravenous. Although they'd given me sufficient nutrition for my needs, I devoured two bars of the granola-like sustenance cubes before I was ready to dress.

Thal had told me to join them in the control room when I was ready. I remembered that he'd said we were approaching Sistema. I wasn't sure what else he told me.

I went to the clothes machine and programmed for the proper clothing. When it ejected, I studied the outfit with dismay. The pants and top were diaphanous. I was not thrilled to have to wear see-through clothes again, and these looked exactly like the slave apparel on Kedor. I shrugged and slipped them on.

There was make-up to put on, too. I painted my eyes and put the patterns on my cheeks that were shown on the diagram given to me by the clothes machine. Then I prepared my hair, tying part of it up into a beehive on top, with the rest dangled down in about twenty slender braids. Ugly!

When I finally arrived in the control room, the males all turned and stared at me, gasping collectively. Five jaws dropped down, and their eyes bugged out. I wished they weren't so blatant in their perusal of me. It made me feel horrid.

"Stars in Heaven, Thalia, what are you doing dressed in Sistema clothing?" Thal asked me, shaking his head in consternation.

"You told me to."

"Thalia, I did not tell you to clothe yourself in Sistema clothing. You are not going down on the planet with us. That would be far too dangerous. I only told you of our arrival because it is safer for you to be awake. Go back to your room immediately and change your clothes. Hair, too. And take that make-up off. You know, Shapechanger do not allow that."

I turned to go. Then, I realized I still didn't know what to wear. "What should I program for?"

"Fregnon."

I turned around and returned to my room. The makeup was not easy to get off, but I changed quickly. Fregnon was very conservative. It was like a gunnysack that wasn't scratchy. I giggled when I thought about the way the male's eyes had popped out. If they thought this was bad, they should have seen the way the Theinian slaver dressed me with breast rouge!

I returned to the control room just as Tren and Thal were leaving.

"You would not have said goodbye?" I asked, close to tears.

Thal gathered me into his arms. "You have slept so much you are saucy as a virgin," he whispered into my ear. "Soon, I shall refresh your memory of dominion."

His lips drove all thoughts of rebellion from my mind. I held on to him like I thought I'd fall off the ship.

When Thal was finished kissing me, he looked down at me and grinned heartily. "Spelon is in charge. You will obey his commands *without* an argument. If I should not return, he is to be your husband. You know what that means, Thalia. There will be no stubbornness about it."

"Please take me with you, *please*!"

"I cannot. Remember what I said. Shaarvan ordered it, Thalia. You will obey his will and mine in this."

The stupid tears were pouring out, streaming like a flooding creek. Stupid hormones.

"I can't, Thal. Please, don't leave me."

"Thalia, I plan to be back. It is only for a while. Spelon, take her."

We had not landed on the planet. The ramp opened only to a spaceport. But it made no difference. Seeing Thal and Tren walk away released more of my floodgate. When the door closed and the screen shut down, I'd already turned in Spelon's arms and was sobbing away.

But tears only last so long. Spelon's shirt was hardly wet when they ran out. I sighed and asked to be freed. Spelon released me and allowed me to go feed Thandar.

The baby and I had a lovely time together. He was all smiles now, and his eyes latched onto me. When I put him down, I peeked in on Thaarac, his toddler brother. Thaarac was sleeping the dreams of the exhausted. He must have just frolicked with one of my bondmates. I kissed him anyway and made my way back to the others.

The three Shapechangers were quiet as a funeral party mourning a beloved. They were playing cards. I sat down beside Tenor and asked if I could join in. He snorted a chuckle and shook his head.

"It is a male's game," Spelon said.

Thedar must have seen that my eyes were tearing up again. "She could play Spitz. There would be no harm in that." He looked over at Spelon for a decision.

Spelon met my eyes. "You will not cry if you lose?"

"Of course not," I said. My chin rose higher, but I was careful not to raise it high enough that he would think I was challenging him.

He considered a moment, glanced at the others, then nodded. "All right," he said, not sounding as gruff as usual.

Thedar began to instruct me on the points of the game. I understood at once. "Then we need chips," I said.

"We play for money, Thalia."

"But I don't have any."

"Do you not know that what is ours is yours?" Tenor said.

"Do not confuse her," Spelon said. "Here, Thalia, take these coins. That will start you off. By the time those are gone, I shall have earned more."

"Not cocky, are you?" Tenor joked.

We began to play, and the time moved so quickly that I hardly noticed its passing. When Tren and Thal returned, I had a whole pile of coins in front of me, and all three Shapechanger owed me more.

Tren laughed when he saw it. "I should have let you work in my casino, Thalia. You would have made me rich!"

"You were already rich," I reminded him.

I was happily scooping up my coins, gloating at the others, when Thal placed his hand on my loot and stopped me. "It is forbidden for a woman to own money. You will give this back."

The three Shapechanger all looked sheepish. They had known all along that I wouldn't be allowed to keep my winnings. I rose up and left the table with what grace I had left, but it rankled me sorely. It was so unfair.

Later, Thal wanted to know why I'd wanted the coins. "Money is for the buying of goods. What goods do you yearn for?" he asked.

I thought about it, but I couldn't think of anything I really wanted except freedom and Shaarvan and things that money couldn't buy. "But it felt good to amass such a pile of it," I said. "I could have kept it for an emergency."

"Money is the power that men crave who have no Mind Power."

"Shaarvan wanted money to buy a ship," I argued.

"His goal of a ship had little value when he lost his wife. He gave it all away to find you."

"Thal, we are about to be boarded," came a voice over the speaker.

Thal punched the orange button. "Get Tren to drug the little ones," he ordered abruptly.

Thal latched onto my hand and pulled me forward. He led me rapidly down the stairs where I'd never been allowed to go. I thought I was keeping up just fine, but he swung me into his arms and ran faster. He didn't stop until he reached a half-port door, which he hand-opened and shoved me into. There was only a shallow cubby beyond, just a bed. He climbed in on top of me and immediately started pulling off my dress.

"Obey me swiftly for your life," Thal ordered. "Do not question me, Thalia. Shapechange now into an image of an older woman with graying hair, uncombed and disheveled. Blacken your teeth and add a stench of rot to your mouth. Good. Now, sag your eyes, wrinkle here, and place a wart, black and shiny, with hair growing out of it. Good girl. Now, the rest of your body, sag it. Fatten your belly and legs. More, Thalia. Pull your breasts down. OK. Now, lie back down. I shall cover you. Do not argue, no matter what I say or do, understand?"

Thal tore off his clothes and acted like a fool. He was on me and pressing his tool inside me when the door slid open.

I screamed and felt Thal's hand slide over my mouth.

"Why do you bother me? I was just getting started with this whore. Leave me." Thal ordered the man staring in at us.

The eyes of the others were surveying me. Thal flew into a rage. "You look at another, you whore!"

Thal slapped me roughly across the face. The blow rocked my head back against the bed and stunned me into a daze of silence.

"Do you wish to watch me take her, or do you have other things to do?" Thal demanded of the man. "Her breath is rancid, and her boobs sag long, but until I can afford another, she services my needs."

The man shook his head and retreated.

"You will not speak or change anything," Thal whispered at me. His hands traveled me, but there was no web. I fought him, incensed by his abuse. Thal brought my arms up and secured them with one hand. His hand roved my body. I was fighting him when the door once again opened.

"I'm going to have to ask you questions, my lord. You'll have to wait on your pleasure with the whore."

Thal grumbled and pulled on his pants. "Move this much," he said to me, showing me a distance with his fingers, "and I shall beat you purple when I return."

The door closed, and I was left alone. I knew that Thal had been playacting, but I was still shaking with my fear. It was too much like my days with Isandor, and Isandor had never called me a *whore*.

It was at least an hour before Thal slipped back in. He sat down on the edge of the cubby and smiled at me. "You may change back now, Thalia," he whispered soothingly.

I studied Thal for a moment. It was difficult to switch instantly from fear of someone to confidence in him. Thal looked the same as before. His dark blond hair, straight and falling into his eyes as he bent over me, was familiar. His long noble nose, the usual half-smile across his mouth . . . Thal's dark craggy eyebrows raised up as I continued staring at him.

"You are frightened of me," he said. His hand gently pushed back my hair and kissed my forehead. His touch didn't ease my apprehension. I began to shake. Thal gathered me into his arms and held me.

"Easy, my wife. I shall not hurt you again. Easy," he said.

With his words and his body pressed to mine, my heart picked up his rhythm, and my trembling stopped. In another moment, I was changing back again. It was so easy. It was like the release of a rubber band that one has pulled taut. I slid back into me and felt waves of relief and well-being. It was like coming home at the end of a long vacation and finding home to be full of comfort and familiarity.

When I had completed the change, Thal took my hand again. "I was rough with you. Forgive me, my dear."

I nodded and looked down. I was still uncertain of him, still a little distrustful of his apology. "Was it me they were searching for?"

Thal was kissing my face. I wished he wouldn't. I wished he'd release my body and back away from me.

"Yes, my dear. Thenos has offered high rewards for his *runaway wife*. It seems you ran off with his son, a babe in arms, who is Thenos' heir and happens to be exactly Thandar's age."

I pulled back in dismay. "But that's all lies. How can a Shapechanger lie? And why has Thenos said those things? Why does he call me his wife and say he has a son?"

"I do not know, but it is interesting that the story calls for your return and not for your death. If all Thenos wanted was revenge on Shaarvan, he could easily have ordered you killed. A wife who runs away from her husband merits death, especially if she has stolen his child. It is obvious Thenos wants you alive. And he wants you untouched, or he would not have given you the title of *wife*. I think Thenos has fallen in love with you."

"Thenos holds no love for anyone."

Thal eyed me a moment as if debating what I'd said.

"No. He has convinced himself so. He puts too much energy into this pursuit of you for it to be anything else, Thalia."

We were still lying in the niche of a bed, with its covers in disarray. It made for cramped quarters with a heavy Shapechanger lord on top. I wiggled restlessly, wanting to ask if we could climb out yet, but I knew that Thal would have done so if it were safe. We must still be in the planet's docking station.

I sighed. I didn't want to think about Thenos. That nightmare of existence had caused my separation from Shaarvan, had injured Tevor, and had killed the children on Westla. He was the horror we were constantly fleeing from.

I fingered my cheek, where my jaw still ached. "Did you have to hit me?"

Thal reached over and touched it. "My child, I am sorry. Forgive me. The guard was looking at your eyes. We should have changed them first, but I did not think of it. Your Power has darkened them to a beautiful metal gray. There is not a doubt when one looks into your eyes that you are Shapechanger, not the slave woman I called you. I could not let the patrol guard see that."

I nodded my head, and I understood. Being Shapechanger, the bruise would disappear quickly. My fear of Thal might take a bit more time, but I had endured worse on Freinana.

"I'm sorry I questioned you, Thal. That guard would have taken me and sent me to Thenos, wouldn't he? Thank you for protecting me."

"Of course, Thalia. But all of us would have defended you. We would die for you. You know that."

I didn't like hearing it, but I knew it was true. Shaarvan had told me so long ago. I nodded.

When Thal folded me into another embrace and kissed my forehead, I concentrated on not retreating.

"Thaarac and Thandar are all right?" I asked.

"They were drugged and hidden. They sleep soundly."

Thal began a pattern on my skin. I couldn't stand it any longer. "Must I stay here?"

"No. Of course not," Thal chuckled. "I shall take you back to our room."

He released me, tore off a sheet from the bed, wrapped me with it, and carried me back upstairs. On the way up, curiosity licked my mind. "Why was I always forbidden to go down there?"

"That area belongs to your bondmates, and they need their privacy from you."

"But it's small and cramped. Couldn't they have better quarters?"

"Privacy means no more questions."

"But . . ."

"You will not mention it again, Thalia."

Thenos

I have been cheated again. When Chaslow arrived at Hershew, the moon of Gerse, they had once again stolen Thenosa away. How have the bondmates felt my soundings? How did they know my discovery of each location? What Powerful Warlord is so attuned to my Power he knows the moment I touch my princess?

Chaslow found their buildings. There was evidence all around they had fled in the night. Vegetables and fruits still lay on the table of the house. Hay had been collected and stored for animals. Several carcasses hung in one of the sheds in preparation for smoking them.

How did they depart so quickly? Chaslow had been only days away from their barbarian planet. He should have seen their ship in his grid. Yet, he did not. And they escaped without a trace as to their destination.

My princess, do you not feel this yearning inside me? You are on my mind day and night. I have built you a palace. I have prepared everything for you. Why do you flee from me? Do you go willingly? Are you that obedient to their will? Or do you scream and cry out in your need for me?

I can almost picture that: your stormy eyes, wild with anger, your teeth clenched or sharply ready to do damage, your slender claws unsheathed, scratching and gouging the males who steal you away from me. Yes, that is how it must be. I know you feel me. I know you lust for my sword.

Do you dream of how it will feel with your warm little body beneath mine? These arms of mine are heavy with muscle. I practice for hours, lifting and pushing up, knowing that I do it for you. I shall ride you long and with ease, my sweet. I shall fulfill all of your needs. Can you imagine how it will be between us?

But I grow tired of waiting. Chaslow has failed again, but I shall not. I shall come to you myself this time. I had thought to do it before, but I allowed Chaslow to attempt one more time. No more. The Royal Barge shall greet the Stars, and I shall find you. Be ready, my princess, my queen.

Chapter Four

Thalia

We were spaced for a manyTide. I grew restless as the Tides flowed by without color. This ship contained no gardens or exercise room with computer-generated play toys, only the treadmill, which we all shared, running on it to keep up our strength.

Once again, Thal joined with me, and our nights found variation in the bliss of union and fulfillment. But my dreams were without Shaarvan, and I began to dread sleep, for the waking from it was so desolate.

Thal was gentle with me at first. He held me and talked, but the loss was too deep. I ached from it increasingly as we traveled farther away from Shaarvan.

Then, like a rubber band stretched too tightly, I snapped and rampaged. It was poor Tren who started it, but it was not his fault, nor Spelon's, who added fuel to the fire. The fault was in my distance from Shaarvan and the fact that he would not allow me to connect with him again.

We were eating breakfast, all together for once. Thandar was sleeping, and Thaarac was playing in his room, so the meal should have been pleasant and peaceful.

It is strange how one moment can change your whole life. One sentence even. Thal called the proceedings that led up to such a solar explosion *a prenova condition*. Perhaps that's what that moment was. All the gases were at critical mass.

I see it as the domino effect. The pieces were all lined up. How innocently we all sat down. Casually, as if it were any old day, yet now, after its conclusion, I look back at it and say that it was the first domino falling.

I remember I had just taken a bite of bread. It wasn't the homemade bread I'd learned to bake on Freinana. It was what the food machine dispensed, and it was dry and tasteless — like most of the food from the ship's dispenser.

Tren still wasn't fully adapted to being Shapechanger. He still said things he shouldn't. I knew that and tried to accept his sometimes hurtful questions. But that time . . .

"What happens when Shaarvan finally joins us?" he asked. "Does Thal stop being Thalia's husband?"

Spit! The silence in that room was as big as if Thenos had just walked in and said, "Hi there, everybody."

"Tren, don't, please," I pleaded, but everyone ignored me. Tren had addressed the question to Thedar. He thought Thedar was the oldest. None of them knew about Thal's true age.

Spelon could never seem to keep his mouth shut. He spoke up first. "Thal has had Thalia longer than Shaarvan ever did. She is Thal's by law."

I wish that at some point in time, I had learned to tune out Spelon, but I never could. The blood drained from my brain, and I was so angry I almost Changed.

I stood up, and my chair fell back. I didn't flinch at the noise of its falling. I probably didn't even hear it. My eyes were only on Spelon. I wanted to throw something at him. I wanted to yell and scream — and push him out the space door. "How dare you!" I yelled at him. "I told you once I shall always be . . ."

"Enough, Thalia. Go to your room." Thal issued the direct command. No warning hand signals, no glaring looks of eyes hardened into concrete.

I meant to obey. I was on my way, almost, but there was a flash of a sneer on Spelon's face, and in his mind, he laughed at me for believing that Shaarvan would ever be able to come back for me.

"You're not a Shapechanger. You're a lowly worm," my mouth cried out, and then I turned and ran.

It sounded like the words of a Terran child, but I had just thrown the gravest Shapechanger insult I knew. I would be punished, of course, but at that moment, I didn't care. I would always hold the memory of Spelon's bloodless eyes as the insult hung there in the air, quivering. I was satisfied.

Thal did not come to me that day. Thedar brought Thandar, and I nursed my baby while the Thedar sat in absolute silence. Before he left, he shook his head at me, and, for the first time, I began to wonder what exactly my punishment would be. Thandar was brought to me throughout the Tide. Each time, Thedar remained silent, nor did he meet my eyes.

When I knew the time had come for sleeping, still Thal did not come. I slept alone that night. It seemed very strange. I had never slept the night without warm arms enveloping me, not since Shaarvan had first captured me. I wondered how long everyone would stay mad at me.

In the wee hours of the morning, Spelon entered my room. I woke up with a sudden premonition of danger. Our eyes met, and I knew instantly that it would be Spelon who doled out the punishment.

"Strip," he ordered me in a voice of gruff determination.

"I am Thal's."

"You are mine for the next day and night."

Once more, I was reminded of how alien the culture of the Shapechanger was to me. I knew their laws held no mercy for women, but I'd always assumed that Thal would do the rendering of any punishment.

I threw my dress down on the floor and stood, proud and seemingly unafraid, although I should have known I was still an open book to the Shapechanger lords. Whatever I was feeling, deep inside, was no mystery to them. But a great act of pseudo-courage was all I had as armor.

Besides, I had known Isandor, and I held the brand of the Shapechanger, the scratches of the Saberey. There was nothing Spelon could do that I could not endure.

"You will beat me, Spelon," I said. "You have wanted to beat me since the first time you met me. It has been in your eyes each time you looked at me. I should have known the inevitability of it. I am prepared. I will not feel it. You cannot hurt me, Warlord. Only tell me what I still do not understand — why did Shaarvan choose you?"

Spelon took a step towards me and flicked a leather strap in the air. I remembered well the pain of it, but I had felt worse. Isandor had used the pain stick on me — and his fists. I would survive Spelon, as I had the rest of the violence. I was beyond trembling and quaking at the feet of Shapechanger.

I rose up taller. My head was high that moment as I faced Spelon. He paused only to take in my nakedness. I did not fear his lust. I had lived through that, too.

"Beat me, Spelon, if it pleases you. Fulfill your needs, but you will not conquer me. I am already conquered. Use the strap to lick my body. I do not fear it or you. I will never recant my words. I am Shaara of Shaarvan."

Like a bull, Spelon roared at me, tossing me back on the bed. The strap bit deeply into my naked thigh. I found the place in the forest where the trees sheltered me, and the wind whistled through their branches. The trees held my aching flesh as the whip descended, and they moaned with their high-pitched whistles, but I felt nothing of Spelon's fury. He could not reach me in my forest. The forest grew still, listening and waiting, then released me. I woke to find Spelon weeping.

"I have not crushed you," he said. "You are like no other female I have ever known. I sought to curb and harness your fire, but it flares still higher. I wanted to tame you for my own, but you are still as unattainable as a mountain crest.

"You asked why Shaarvan gave you to me as a third. His words were this. 'You can never own Shaara, but she will teach you how to love.' I thought he mocked me. I am a soldier, although I am highborn like the others. I thought I knew all there was of women, but Shaarvan was right — my heart is full of you. My throat is parched from struggling not to say the words. My skin is burned from craving your touch. I ache in the night, but no other fulfillment can relieve my lust for you.

"Every word I threw at your heart, I wounded you with because of your love of Shaarvan. I thought there was no depth to a woman, but I find the depths inside me are shallow in comparison to the reaches of your inner soul. You are a warrior, Thalia, a warrior with the fierceness of your love and your unending strength to endure. I am truly but a worm at your feet."

I had crushed him. Tears came to my eyes, not from the beating but from his words. I cried out, "Spelon, I am sorry. I should not have called you that, but you made me so angry. My anger is a child. I don't have the wisdom to contain it. Please, forgive me."

Spelon stood over the bed, looking down at me. He shook his head in wonder.

"Five times, I whipped this leather across your body and saw your skin writhe in pain. The wounds of my vengeance have marred the perfection of your delicate skin, and you ask for *my* forgiveness? What warrior would not be filled with hatred by such abuse?"

"You called me a warrior falsely, Spelon. I would fight to protect my loved ones, but don't you see, Spelon, you are one of them."

He sighed, long and heavy, then wagged his weighty head. "I had planned to rape you through the night and day. It would have been a crime against Shapechanger values, but I thought that then you would learn to give me deference. I think if I did that you would only respect me less. I envisioned pleasing myself and claiming you as a war trophy, but I can do that no longer."

I said nothing. There was no adequate response to his words.

"You would not have fought me, I think. You would have closed off into your forest, and I would have spilled my sterile seed inside you, but you would not have felt it, and for all the days that come, I would lust for you like a drowning man who craves air. I do not know how Thal has endured it, but I could not. Nor could I bear your hatred."

I touched Spelon's arm and drew his eyes back to me. "I do not know if I would fight you, Spelon, but Shaarvan owns my heart. Only Shaarvan sings my song.

"Tren told me once that I drove Isandor mad because of my untouchable essence. Isandor was a man who thought he could possess a Shapechanger. Thal is Shapechanger. He has more of me than Isandor, but it is not enough for him either. Of late, I can barely tolerate his touch."

"I want no part in raping you, Thalia. I was wrong to beat you. Talk to me, little warrior. Tell me of Shaarvan and how he was able to gain your heart."

Spelon brought a dress from the clothes machine. It was a blue one, the color women wore in his land. I wore it to please him. He spread salve on my welts tenderly, apologizing for my pain.

Then he sat down on the bed beside me, and I talked of Shaarvan, the way he'd captured me, the way our life had been before my adaptation. I explained that it was still a mystery to me how I could have given him my heart when his cruelty was beyond measure.

"He took you in the Old Way. That is what bonded you so deeply. You are soul-bonded, a link of permanence," Spelon said. "It would be death for either of you to sever that connection. Now, I understand. Forgive me."

After a while, Spelon left me and went to get us food. The machine in the room only delivered nutrition bars. Neither of us had the stomach for that.

When Spelon returned with a meal, we ate, laughing over our crumbs and other silly things. Thedar brought in my sons and sat with us for a time. He asked no questions, but I think he was relieved to see that I was okay. He handed Spelon some more salve, in case it was needed, but said nothing about my punishment.

After Thedar left with Thandar, Spelon asked again for my permission to apply the medicine. Once more, I raised my dress, and he laid me down on my stomach. It stung as he coated all the welts, but it was not the stinging that worried me. I was afraid that with his hand touching me, Spelon would change his mind. Yet, when Spelon finished, I put my dress back on, and it was as it had been before.

The day unwound slowly, like being snowed in for a weekend with someone. You shared things you didn't normally share, and a closeness developed from our confinement.

I fell asleep at one point and slept for hours. When I woke, Spelon's eyes were still wide awake. I knew he had not slept at all. "Aren't you tired?" I asked.

"When it is time for me to go, then I shall sleep, for then I shall no longer feel I have the right to meet your eyes as freely or watch you — soaking in the color of your hair, the delicacy of your skin, the silky lengths of your eyelashes. I shall never again be at your side watching the innocence of your sleep. You look like Thaarac when you sleep, except you do not suck your thumb."

I laughed, as he meant me to. What else could I do?

Spelon left me in the wee hours of the morning. I was so sleepy that I almost didn't say goodbye.

It couldn't have been much later when Thal entered. His arms surrounded me, and he held me close. "I am sorry for the necessity of that," he said. "How badly did Spelon hurt you?"

I shrugged and said, "I will survive, but I am very tired. May I sleep?"

"Poor kid." I felt Thal's lips kiss my forehead before I drifted off.

In the morning, Thal insisted on seeing the welts. He whistled when he saw them. "He was not gentle, Thalia, but he could have hurt you worse."

"No, Thal. He could not," I said. "There was nothing Spelon could do that hurts me worse than being far from Shaarvan."

Thal studied my eyes. "Spelon drove you up another level. Did you not feel the strap at all?"

"No. The forest held me and covered my pain. Spelon could not reach me, nor could Thenos."

Thal bolted up. "What has Thenos to do with this?"

"I must go to Thenos. Spelon says that I am a warrior, but I told him I would only protect the ones I love. That is the solution. I must kill Thenos before he hurts the ones I love."

Thal's eyes darkened. His cheekbone writhed with tension. "Thalia, never say that again. I shall beat you worse than Spelon has if you ever mention meeting Thenos again.

"I will go to the forest and come back when you are through, and then I will say it again."

"Stars in Heaven! I did not believe that Spelon would push you into outright rebellion."

"I will obey you, Thal, but the war needs a catalyst. It goes on and on. Thenos knows it. That is why he searches for me."

"If Thenos ever catches you, I have vowed to kill you. Shaarvan made us all pledge that."

"Then kill me, but let me kill Thenos first."

"You do not understand."

"Why do Shapechanger males say that so often and then choose not to explain?"

"Because some of our women do not think!"

Thal left me, storming away. His anger lingered in the room long after he was gone. I had barely gotten back to sleep when he returned. "You did not tell me that Spelon did not take you."

"You never asked."

"I worried so that he would hurt you, and I did not wish to tread on such a delicate matter."

"It didn't bother you when you gave me to Spelon," I said, careful to modulate my voice but leave the sting of the words.

Thal raised his hand as if to slap me, but he lowered it and said, "Strip."

The blue dress of Spelon's choice was quickly on the floor. I wondered how I could so easily go from one potential rape to another.

"Rape, it will not be, Thalia. You have shown me how easy it is for you to escape. I shall make you feel this."

Thal placed webs on me. I was surprised. He had not used those since Deadstar. The patterns followed, and then he drove me into desire.

But then he stopped and looked down at me. "Thalia, I shall no longer share you. Spelon is correct. You are mine legally now. I shall stop this nonsense of yours. I know things that Shaarvan did not, and one of them is how to break his soul binding."

Thal's eyes were red with jealousy. Had I driven him mad like I had Isandor?

"Please, do not do that, Thal. You promised Shaarvan that you would take care of me, that you would never hurt me. Thal, please, don't break my bond with Shaarvan, please! I can endure anything except that."

"You are only a woman, Thalia. You will accept it. And then, you will be mine."

"Wait," I begged him. "Spelon said that Shaarvan and I were death bonded."

Thal laughed. "That is a fantasy of the Old Ones. There is no truth in it." His lips cut off any further words. With his fingers, Thal began a new pattern. I wanted to fight it, but I was webbed in so tightly I couldn't move. My eyes pleaded, but Thal wasn't listening or reading my thoughts. His finger traced the pattern over and over, burning it into my skin. I moaned from the agony.

"It works," Thal gloated.

His eyes had taken on a feverish look. "You will never shut me out again, Thalia," he said.

"You're hurting me, Thal."

"Yes, I know," he laughed. "Feel me, Thalia. Feel the pain. It is the brand I place on you. It is I you will cry out for in the night. It is I your soul will hunger for."

When Thal took me, there was great pain. I screamed, and then he drove into me. It was not rape. I wanted him desperately. I needed him. The release sent us sailing upwards into the sky. I felt the bond tighten, and I knew that Thal had succeeded in placing a new soul bonding. Why did I feel only emptiness and loss?

Thal lifted up off of me. I bore the numbness of the Shapechanger snow. I felt like a wild mustang that had run free until the rope came slinging out over his head, spinning in circles to fall and grab my neck. There was no pleasure in my bonding with Thal. There was only an empty space in my heart where I'd once felt Shaarvan.

Thal snored gently, content with his success. I analyzed what I was sensing. Something was wrong. Thal had achieved his soul binding, but he'd broken something inside me. I didn't understand the awareness of it, but I knew that Shaarvan had never lied to me. Spelon had told me about the death bond. They were right.

When Thal woke, he sat up to look at me. His eyes were still wild. I do not believe he read my soul or looked inside me. He only saw someone he'd just conquered.

"Look happy, woman. I order you."

"I do not feel well, Thal. I think something went wrong."

He scoffed coldly. "You are a melodramatic child. I have pampered you for far too long. Many things will change now. First, I shall never hear the name of your first husband again. He is dead."

"How could you demand that of me?" I wailed.

Thal slapped me hard across the face. My lip stung. I tasted blood where my tooth had cut the lip. Thal's eyes, as they stared down at me, were the eyes of Isandor.

"Answer me, or I shall hit you again."

"I cannot do as you command."

Again, the hand came down. I felt my lip swelling already from the first slap.

"Perhaps I, too, must bind you in the Old Way. Will you obey me better with scratches tearing open your arms? Perhaps my teeth shall rend your lovely skin. Compliance, Wife."

I could not win. And it no longer mattered. If what Shaarvan and Spelon had told me was true, I was dying anyway. I lowered my head. "Compliance," I said.

Thal took me to eat with the others. As we walked in, Tren bolted up, glaring at Thal. The others urged him down. I wanted to tell them it was not important. Nothing mattered anymore.

Thal ordered me to eat. I could barely move my lips. I could not get the food between them. I looked down, wondering if Thal would beat me for not eating. I no longer cared.

I remember how I'd thought the first time I saw the ship's food heated that it was worms. They had wiggled so. I had tried to run away, and Shaarvan had been so angry with me.

"Thalia, you were asked a question," Thal broke into my thoughts.

"I'm sorry. I did not hear," I said. I wasn't sure if they could understand me. My lips were caking stiffly.

"I asked if you would like ice for your lip. It seems to be bleeding." Thedar asked.

I tried to smile at him, but I could not. "Please ask Thal," I said. "I do not know."

Shaarvan allowed me to try all the different foods by number on the food machine. He'd mocked me often, but he'd been proud of my efforts. One dish had been so horrible I couldn't eat it. I remember how Shaarvan had traded with me. Then he'd smiled at me with his dimples. His smile was such a lovely smile. Would he allow me to say "lovely?" No, I would say charismatic . . .

"Thalia."

I looked up. Why were they all staring at me? Had I done something wrong? Shaarvan had not allowed the crew to stare. They hadn't noticed me at all. I remembered the time I'd focused on the men, trying to get them to react to me. Shaarvan had been very angry.

"Thalia, what is wrong?"

Thedar was touching me. Was he allowed to? Would Shaarvan be angry with him? Once, Shaarvan had let me dance with men, but he had been so jealous afterward. He had licked my body all over, making sure I was fully his again.

"She is in shock," Tren said.

Tren? Why was Tren here? Shaarvan had not been that angry with him for kissing me. He'd told Tren he would find him a wife . . .

Why was Tren carrying me? Was I still on Freinana? Tren was stepping over Thal. Why was Thal on the floor? Spelon had a pipe drawn. Why would he draw his pipe on Thal? They must be playing. Males were so silly.

Tren did not have furry hair like Shaarvan. His hair felt like hair. I wondered why Shaarvan's was so soft.

"Where are you hurt, Thalia?" Tren asked me.

"Hurt?"

"What did Thal do to you?" Spelon demanded.

"He broke me. I will die now."

"Thalia, how did he break you?" Thedar asked.

"He broke my soul binding with — I can't say his name."

"With Shaarvan?"

I nodded. "Thal will beat you for saying his name."

"Shaara, listen to me. I think you have to talk to Shaarvan. It is very important. You must tell him what Thal did. Can you do that?" Thedar asked.

"No."

"Why not? Are you out of range?"

"Range? I don't think that matters."

"Shaara, you must talk to Shaarvan."

"Shaarvan won't let me."

"Shaara, we are your bondmates. We command you to do this."

"But Shaarvan told me not to."

"He told you to obey us. Do it, Shaara. Contact Shaarvan now." Spelon demanded.

I closed my eyes and thought about the comet that had first taken me to Shaarvan. I thought about Shaarvan and how much I loved him. *Shaarvan, Shaarvan, Shaarvan, Shaarvan,* I called.

It was harder to hold him, but he knew me. He was angry at my disobedience. *Please, Shaarvan,* I said. *My bondmates ordered me to tell you that Thal broke my soul bond. I think I am dying.*

160

Thal could not have done so, Shaara.

I cannot eat, and I am empty and lost.

*Stars, Shaara! I feel it now. There **is** a wrongness. Shaara, we are still joined in other ways. I can feel your love. I can feel the warmth of it in my mind. I will hold onto a strand of It will bridge us across the stars. It will guide me to you. I shall come for you, but you must hold on, Shaara, my soul. Promise me. Promise me that you will not slip away.*

I promise, Shaarvan. I will wait for you. I will wait for you forever.

Try to force the food into you, Shaara. You will not live to see me if you do not. If the food will not stay down, they will have to give you nutrient injections. I shall come in the fastest ship. I still have the Westlan ship. I love you. Wait for me . . .

Tenor

None of us can believe what Thal did. He must be mad. There is no other explanation. He would never have hurt Thalia otherwise. We had often commented about his patience and gentleness with the girl. To turn on her and beat her . . . Why?

Poor child, her lip was cut and bleeding. She could barely move it. Thal must have used his fist on her. How could he have done that? We all knew how fragile Thalia's bones were, how incapable she was of defending herself. We cherished her. We protected her. What had caused such a thing?

I knew that Thalia would heal. Her eyes, puffy from tears and desperation, would soon be sparkling once again. She was Shapechanger. A day or so, and she would once more be pleasing to the eye. But something nagged at my surety. Something alarmed us even more than the bruises on her face.

It was her eyes. They had faded. They were dull and almost blue. And her mind was wondering. She had not been able to control its drifting from scene to scene with Shaarvan. Her passivity — that is what had worried me the most. I had never seen her like that. I had never believed that Thalia could be listless. Something was very wrong.

Tren had been the one to move on Thal. He had recognized that Thalia had been mistreated. Why had we not realized it? Why had we continued to sit and ask her questions that she seemed unable to answer?

Would we have interfered? It was so ingrained in us that a husband had the right to govern his wife. Would we have had the good sense to overrule Thal? I think Tren saved her life. It was as the Old Ones said. They sent Tren to save Thalia. He told us that, but we did not believe it.

Why had I not seen Thalia's danger? None of us had reacted as true bondmates. We had not protected her. We had merely asked her questions and pretended not to see the abuse.

Spelon seized his pipe gun, but too late — Tren had already picked her up.

Why had I not rushed in to save the girl? I would never forgive myself for letting her down. Poor Thalia. I love you, little one.

Thalia

I have talked with Shaarvan, and he is coming! Suddenly, I wanted to live. A wild joy filled my body, and I did not believe I would ever need sustenance again. The knowledge of Shaarvan's coming would suffice.

But, obedient to the will of Shaarvan, I returned to the table. I tried to eat. The food was like paste — thick and tasteless. I could barely swallow. It was as if I had forgotten how.

Spelon mashed some preserved fruits for me until it looked like the food Shaarac used to eat for his meals, but I could not eat it. Tren thinned it still more and made it into a drink. The eyes of the Shapechanger urged me. I swallowed most of the liquid, but after a while, I was sick, and it all came up. I knew then that I would have to take the injections Shaarvan had ordered.

"I have some, Shaara, but not much," Tren told me. "We used it while you were asleep with the Shawl."

"I can last a while without it," I told him, feeling still a kind of floating buoyancy from Shaarvan's contact.

Tren would not listen. He shook his head and said, "No. You are still in shock. We cannot risk it."

So the injections started, and I felt marvelous. I was so light and cheerful that I thought all the gloom in the ship would be dispelled, but my smiles were not reflective. The Shapechanger all around me were worried and sad, and their faces dragged.

They had taken Thal to his computer chamber and locked him in there. They told me he was well and was sorry for what he had done to me. I could not hate him anymore. I had driven him to. It was the same madness as Isandor's.

I knew my lip would heal before Shaarvan came. My bruises always disappeared before their time, and the truth of it was that I should be thankful to Thal for forcing Shaarvan to return.

I felt that I should visit Thal. He had husbanded me gently for a long time. We had been together for almost two Passes, but he had severed that. I did not know if I could bear the sight of him.

I could no longer nurse Thandar. My milk had dried up with Thal's breaking of my bond. I gave the baby a bottle, and I held him and kissed him, but although he was all smiles and sweet adorableness, something else had dried up inside me. I could no longer love Thandar. I knew my bondmates loved him. They would foster all his needs.

I worried about Thaarac. How would he take the loss of Thal and the arrival of Shaarvan? And what would Shaarvan say when he discovered that Thaarac did not even know his rightful name or his true father?

I tried to explain to my son that he would no longer be called Thaarac, but he called me *Silly Mommy* and would not sit to hear my words. I was not surprised. They had trained him well to be a Shapechanger.

I spent most of my time with my bondmates, attempting to gather information about weapons and how to curb my own unmanageable projection. It was Thedar who finally helped me tone my thoughts. It had all been so easy once it was explained. I simply had to muzzle them. It was like learning to Shapechange with my clothes on: Hold on to them, Thal had told me. Such an easy thing when you knew what to do.

My projection was the same as that. I practiced loud and soft, throwing my thoughts to other rooms where a bondmate could receive them and hiding my thoughts next to a Shapechanger where he could not pick them up. It was a game to them. They did not realize how important the knowledge was to me.

Information about weapons was far more difficult to pursue. Spelon was not easy to get information from in any area. He always questioned my need for it. I thought that sweet words would pry it from him, but we had grown too close.

He laughed at me when I tried the flattery and said, "Weapons are a male thing, Shaara. Shaarvan would not thank me for broadening your education in that manner."

Tenor laughed at me, too, when I went to him, and Thedar's response was almost the same. There was only Tren to ask — Tren, who knew me better than I knew myself.

He didn't bother to answer my questions. He called for all of my Bondmates except Thal and dragged me to the table. He was gentle as he pushed me into the chair, but his gentleness was firm. "Give, Shaara. What are you up to?"

The males sat down as seriously as if it were a battle tactics discussion. I suppose that, in a way, it was. What a shock it would be for them to find that I planned to be the general. I looked around the circle of faces, and my eyes softened.

They were good Shapechanger, all of them, and I loved each one of them. My son, Shaarac, my beloved husband — what more could a person desire than all those that were held in the heart? I allowed my feelings to be projected. I felt the melting of the hardness in their eyes.

Each one of them swayed into what I felt. Tenor and Thedar looked like they would cry. Spelon couldn't meet my eyes. He stared up at the ceiling.

Only Tren broke the warmth. Tren had sat in the circle, but he seemed immune, and he was glaring at me. Tren's eyes looked around him and came back angrier. "Enough, Shaara. I am about to turn you over my knee. You will not turn your force on us, Woman."

His rage blasted me, and I lost my hold on the others. Freed, they, too, turned angry eyes at me.

Thedar spoke first. "Our shields were down because we trusted you. You are ours as we are yours. Yet you were false with us?"

Four sets of hard, cold eyes accused me. I looked each of them in the eyes and saw their recriminations.

"Forgive me," I sobbed. I could not stand to see them disappointed in me. "I was not false. It is how I feel, but I projected it. I didn't know it would work so well. Please, do not be angry with me. I will not do it again."

Again, their eyes softened. "There is only one woman who has the Power to do what you just did, Shaara. She is the Old One, Tessa." Tenor spoke as if he merely said his thoughts. "How high are you now?"

"I do not know. Thal said I was probably an eight or a nine."

"Spit on Barquel!" Spelon said.

Tren and I looked at each other and started to laugh. "You sound like a Freinanan!" I told Spelon as he became irritated with our laughter.

He growled at us and, ignoring our comment and said. "That kind of Power does not belong in a woman."

"Shaara comes the way she is, Spelon," Tren said with a shrug.

Tren's eyes focused on me. I was stunned he was using Shapechanger Power. I could not look away.

"You are hiding something, Shaara. You were practicing that projection with the same determination you have used to pester us about weapons. What I want to know is why you were practicing, and what is it, this time, that rules your conniving brain?"

Four Shapechanger Warrior lords sat at the table, surrounding me with their hugeness, their immense Power, and their masculine air of dominance, but I saw only my three guardians and Tren — the males who had befriended me and sheltered me through endless turmoil. I would miss them when I departed from this plane.

Then, I stirred my thoughts to encounter Tren's words. Why was it that I was conniving and pestering when I only wanted things that were normally given out freely — to males?

He didn't wait for me to deal with the rush of rebellion that suddenly filled me with a boost of Power.

"Out with it, Shaara, or you will feel four male minds probing you."

It was not a nice threat. I rose and backed away. "I am not conniving, and I don't pester. If none of you will help me, I will . . . I will ask Thal."

Tren bolted up. "No, you will not! You will stay away from him." It was a command. Again, Tren had taken charge. His body blocked my retreat. His hand slid around my neck.

"Tren!" I cried out in exasperation, reeling from the impact of his treachery.

"Sit down," he ordered me.

"She wants to take on Thenos," Tenor said quietly.

I hadn't felt Tenor's probe. How had he discovered the thought?

"That fits. I knew she was up to something," Tren said. He did not remove his hand from my neck.

"Every male on Altar is in a full battle against this Thenos, and you think that you, a woman, can accomplish what they cannot?" Spelon jeered.

It was too late to hide from them. They wouldn't allow me to keep anything from them now, so I answered Spelon.

"Yes. I do."

"You would be safer nude in my casino," Tren threw at me. He flashed a *stay command*. I nodded in compliance. Then, I sighed with relief as his hand dropped from the hated neck grip.

"How, Shaara?" Thedar wanted to know. "Tell us."

I smiled at him, thankful that at least one of them was willing to listen. "The war needs a catalyst. It drags on and on, and both sides seem evenly matched. Thenos keeps calling for me. He knows I have Power, but he doesn't know how much. He thinks I'm just a slave girl that Shaarvan married."

"You are," Spelon said. Then, as if remembering our recent conversation, he sputtered. "No, Shaara, that's not true."

"Spelon, you said I was a warrior."

Tenor stood up, towering over Spelon. "I have warned you to guard your tongue around Shaara."

"Enough," Tren demanded abruptly. His eyes once more held mine. They were green with Power. It was difficult to concentrate on what he was saying. "Shaara, I am trying to understand your thinking. Clarify this for me. You wanted us to tell you about weapons so you could kill Thenos with one?"

His eyes shaded to gray. The intensity of his Power had varied, freeing me from his internal perusal. For the first time, I recognized his kinship with Shaarvan. I knew that flare of Power, recognized it. A Trendacons' Power cycled through the Saberey. It might be only at the beginning stage, but Tren would be a force to reckon with. He would be another Shaarvan, a Tevor, a Thenos.

I swallowed and answered, "No, Tren, shooting Thenos wouldn't work. He would know I had a weapon. I want to have a gun, so he will take it away from me. He will assume then that I am defenseless."

"Female reasoning," Spelon said, shaking his head. "You would be defenseless."

Tren shot him a look.

"Without a weapon, how would you kill Thenos?" Thedar asked, ignoring Spelon.

I met each of their eyes. I must be strong enough to convince them yet offer them no challenge to provoke their Shapechanger authority.

"If my Power is great enough, and if Thal will give it to me, there is a potion. When I drink it, I will be a High Priestess like Tessa."

"No." Three Shapechanger voices denounced my idea. Tenor's and Thedar's faces Changed. For them to lose control like that, my statement had riled them gravely. I shot a quick glance at Spelon. He wasn't at the point of Change, but he was glaring at me, although his eyes held more uncertainty than anger.

Tren remained silent, staring at them. "I do not have that knowledge, Shaara. Tell me about being a High Priestess. Do you mean like Tessa? What would copying her have to do with Thenos?"

Thedar's eyes did not let go of me. "It is a lonely life, Shaara. No husband, no children, no friends. Would you truly choose that?"

Each word he said was an arrow piercing my soul, but a meaningless one. I was dying. I would soon enough be of little use to a husband, children, or friends. There was only one way I could make my life count, and I would give everything to save those I loved. Nothing else mattered.

"I would not choose to be a Priestess if things were different."

"Shaara," Tren warned.

I turned my eyes to him. I started to answer his question, but Tenor said the words first. "A High Priestess can kill with her thoughts."

"You cry when they cut down a tree. How in Barquel do you expect to kill a man?" Tren asked me.

"Shapechanger," Tenor corrected.

I didn't wait for Tren to understand Tenor's correction. I went on. "A woman learns to endure, to bear what she must. I can kill if it is to protect my own."

"Shaarvan will not permit it. We are wasting our time debating this. Shaara is a woman. She will do as her husband tells her," Spelon reminded everyone.

"I will need your help with that, Spelon," I said. "I will need the help of all of you. I cannot drink the potion in my weakened condition. I must wait for Shaarvan. And you are right. He will not permit it. You must all make sure he does not stop me."

"Shaara, you are as mad as Thal," Tren said. "None of us will come between you and Shaarvan. It is his right to forbid you."

"Then you are fools!" I said, springing up. "Thenos and I shall meet. I know it is true. I have seen it in my visions. If you do not help me prepare, he will kill Shaarac and Shaarvan — and all the rest of us."

"We would kill you before we let Thenos have you," Spelon reminded me. The haughty look on his face was the same one he'd worn before our talk in Thal's room. Had he forgotten everything we'd shared during our day and night together?

"No," I said, shaking my head, sighing because I'd actually counted on his support. "I know you have all vowed to do that, but in my vision, there is just Thenos and me."

"You see what you want to see, nothing more. It is only the dreams of a woman," Spelon said.

He looked slightly less certain of his words but not enough to count. Would they all stand against me, defeat me in the only plan that would work?

"Would you say that to Tessa?" I asked, turning to the others to look at them eye to eye. The Power in me grows. What I see is a true vision. I will be a Priestess soon."

Thedar's eyes revealed that he was listening, considering my words.

"I have long known that you were one of the Highest, Shaara," he said. "There has always been that about you. But think well before you take that step. A High Priestess has always been one of great age, one who has already *lost* her mate. Are you ready to give up Shaarvan?"

It was Thedar that I addressed then. I saw in his eyes that I was winning him over. "I have no choice. Thenos and I will meet soon. It is not of my choosing."

"Women do not fight wars," Spelon chipped in again, unable to accept that I was going to be the one to end Thenos' life.

"So war is a game which only males may play?" I asked, not even looking his way. I had lost him. I knew that, but Tenor, Thedar, and Tren might still be swayed.

Spelon growled.

I met his eyes fully then. "Spelon," I said, as softly as I could, hoping to remove the sting from my words, "when I talked with Shaarvan through the stars, I saw that this war does make use of its women. Teea, Shaarvan's mother, is using the Power she has to bolster their defense."

I turned to all of them. "Shaarvan has not seen the changes in me. I love him. None of you can doubt that, but he will still see me as the girl he took from Earth, frightened and rebellious but obedient to his strength. I remember that girl, but it's not who I am now. Now, I am a warrior, as Spelon said. He will tell you that I cannot feel pain when I retreat inside me, and you all know that I have the strength to bring my death at will."

"None of us doubt that," Tenor said. "For a woman, you have great Power, but you are young . . ."

172

"I have two sons . . ."

Thedar waved me silent. "You are young in Passes, Shaara, which means you are young in wisdom and in the making of decisions. Yet, we are gathered around you, a woman, and we are listening to you. The Power in you is indeed strong."

Again, I started to say something, but his hand flashed the silence command.

He looked around the table at the others, and his eyes fell on Spelon. "Tren has taken on your rights, Spelon. He commands Shaara as if he were her mate, but the right is yours, Spelon. You are now her Second. You must make the decisions for Shaara.

"Spelon, do we give Shaara the knowledge of weapons that she desires? Do we teach her as if she were to go to war? Perhaps Shaarvan would wish this. I doubt he will leave her again, and if she goes with him to Altar, maybe she would need the knowledge we seek to withhold from her."

"Yes. Tenor is right," said Thedar. "We may discuss it, but the decision is Spelon's. Shaara belongs to him until Shaarvan arrives."

I sighed my anger. I hated the way that Tenor had taken away my rights with one flash of his hand. I could have argued and fought it, but I had temporarily lost my bid for Power. Until I was a High Priestess, they were still my lords.

"You are correct. I should not have stepped forward," Tren said, but he looked doubtful. He met my eyes, but he spoke to the others. "She is Spelon's by Shaarvan's command. I, too, shall stand by Spelon's decisions."

For the hundredth time, no, the thousandth time, I wished that Shaarvan had made any of the others back-up to Thal. I sighed again and lowered my head. I already knew what Spelon would say.

"Come here, woman, and look at me," Spelon ordered.

I obeyed, but there was no trembling in me when I looked up at my new lord. I met his eyes fully, not in challenge, but not in fear either. Spelon probed me deeply but without any pain. I was surprised he was so considerate. A sudden memory flashed in my mind of how it had been that night when we'd talked. I remembered his tenderness with the babies and how he was Shaarac's favorite.

Spelon nodded once and then withdrew. He raised his hand and stroked my cheek. "I would have been equally gentle in the taking of you, Shaara. A warrior also needs to understand devotion."

"You will not take her," Tren said, springing up from his chair.

"That is my decision," Spelon announced, angry at the challenge. Yet he did not remove his hand from my cheek nor look at Tren as if the Shapechanger's rage were an impediment to his decision. Instead, Spelon continued to regard me with his full attention.

I raised my eyes to meet his. I had gone beyond resentment, disappointment, or challenge. No matter what was decided, I knew the outcome. I would kill Thenos with or without the assistance of my bondmates.

Once more, Spelon stroked my cheek, then he sighed. "No, I shall not take her, Tren. She is Shaarvan's. She has always been his."

"And?" Tenor asked.

Spelon nodded. "She is a warrior. We shall train her. If Shaarvan is displeased, he should not have given her to a Warrior. For battle is what I know best."

Thal

I could not have done what they said I did. I would never have hurt Thalia. I loved her. I still do.

Tenor said that her lip was torn and swollen, so that she could no longer smile or speak. But I have no memory of hitting her. I would never have used my fist.

They say I did worse yet. They say I broke her bond with Shaarvan. That I admit. Of course, I broke her bond. The time had come for her to stop her childishness about him. Thalia was my wife, not Shaarvan's. She had borne me a son. She had melded her body to mine. Why should I not have forged our bond more deeply? Surely, it was my right.

Tenor told me that Thalia was sick because of it. But she could not be sick. She is Shapechanger. Tenor must be mistaken. Thalia will grow more beautiful, and then they will see. Her eyes will shine when she sees me. She will lay her hand in mine and crawl into my lap. She knows her owner. Soon, she will beg me to take her again.

It was Spelon who did this. Spelon wanted her. He turned them against me. But Thalia does not yearn for Spelon. She fears him. She will never turn to him. She will cry out my name, and then I shall go to her, and all will be well.

You will see.

Shaara

It was not only a period of waiting then but of preparation. The Shapechangers were united in training me. Spelon introduced me to various weapons. I learned how to use them and how to refill their empty panels when the charge was low. I was not allowed to fire them, which I argued with Spelon over. But on that, he would not waver.

"If you need to use a weapon, you will point it, and you will shoot it. There is nothing more."

I suppose that made sense. But in my home world, there were gun classes and shooting ranges. I remembered seeing targets set up, and in old movies, cowboys practiced on tin cans.

"But don't I need to practice aiming?" I asked, making sure I understood.

"It is against Altarian law for a woman to hold a weapon. I do not think that the law has changed. If you shoot this shortpipe, it will only be because the enemy attacks you personally. I cannot envision that, Shaara. We shall always be there protecting you. However, if . . ."

For a moment, Spelon stopped and looked fully into my eyes. Then he continued. "If Thenos were to win through to you, and we had all Passed to a different plane, then you must aim the shortpipe here, Shaara," Spelon said, pointing at my head. "You will not need to practice that, little warrior. Just do it quickly."

My visions had told me that it would not happen that way. I think Spelon knew it, too, but he would not allow himself to think of Thenos taking the shortpipe from me. It didn't matter, really. I only wanted the knowledge of how to shoot it lying in my brain for Thenos to read. I already knew Thenos' Power was too strong for me to ever use a shortpipe near him. I only needed a block to hide my Power. When Thenos took my only weapon, I would cry, and thus, he would be assured I was conquered.

Spelon began to teach me a form of fighting that was like Terran karate. He and I both knew that there was no time for me to gain competence, but Spelon believed that the warrior stances would aid my mental discipline. I was eager to learn them.

It took me a week, but I finally gained the courage to face Thal. Thedar came with me, as did Spelon. They said nothing of Tren's ordering me not to go near my former husband. Besides, Spelon had decided it was time to confront one of my demons, as he called Thal, and it was Spelon's decision that counted.

Thal rose when he saw me. His eyes no longer looked mad with jealousy. He started to come closer, but Thedar ordered him to stay back.

Thal stood quietly. His eyes pulled at my soul. They were the eyes of a man who had just killed his wife in a jealous rage and wakens to see her in front of him.

"I am sorry, Thalia. Forgive me," he said.

I did not correct him in his naming of me. He was almost as broken as I was.

"They keep telling me you are dying," Thal said. "Do they lie? You will not lie to me, Thalia. Tell me the truth."

"I already did, Thal. I told you what Shaarvan had said. He and I are death-bonded. It was the truth. I am dying. I can no longer eat. The food will not stay down."

Thal screamed like a Banshee. He stomped the floor, turned in a circle, and whirled around to look at me. "Thedar, tell me that isn't true. She looks okay, thinner a bit, but still okay."

I had stepped back. His man scream had startled me. It wasn't like Thal. He'd always been so calm, so patient.

Thedar's arm swept around my shoulder. He seemed ready to lift me out of the room if necessary. Behind me, Spelon was growling softly, his Change near the surface.

"Shaara does not lie, Thal. Shaarvan is on his way. He will save her."

Of course, there was more to Thedar's sentence that he did not add. Shaarvan would save me, save both of us, if he arrived in time. Perhaps Thal did not read that from my mind or the others. Or, maybe he didn't want to.

"I did not believe that breaking the bond would hurt you, Thalia," Thal said. "I thought it would only make you mine."

"I know, Thal."

The dominoes had fallen, and there was no rectifying their positions. Maybe they'd dissolved into the table where the game had been played or been tossed out into space. I suppose that Tessa would have said that everything was occurring just as it was supposed to.

But like the dominoes, I, too, had fallen. Only scattered pieces of me would remain for Shaarvan, Thenos, the guardians, and my sons.

I feared that too many pieces would be gone. Would I still be able to do what I must?

"I have read through all my books, searching for a way to undo it," Thal continued. "But I can find nothing."

"Shaarvan is coming. We won't let her die," Spelon said, his voice husky from his half-Change.

"Stars! Thalia. I only meant to make you mine."

"I know, Thal," I said again.

Thal took a step closer, reaching out his arms to hold me, I think.

"Back off," Thedar repeated. "You are not to touch her. Not ever again."

Thal nodded, even before he noticed Spelon moving forward, this time in full Change. A Saberey nose propelled itself into my left hand. I stroked his fur.

"Of course," Thal said, addressing Thedar's order. "But you understand, Thalia? I did not mean to hurt you. It was only training."

"I understand," I said, but I remembered what Thal had done to my lip, and I shuddered.

"I would not have hurt you more. I would not have been Isandor. I would have loved you, Thalia. I love you still."

I said nothing. Thedar kissed my forehead. Spelon rubbed my side with his massive head. They gave me their strength.

"Thal, it is done," I said.

"Yes. I have killed you. You, the one I loved more than the stars themselves, I have killed you."

I was sorry I had driven him to this state. Had it been my fault? I'd told Thal from the first I loved Shaarvan. What could I have done differently?

Thal turned to glare at Thedar. "She will steal your dreams, Thedar. Do not let her."

"It was not your fault, Shaara. He is Shapechanger. He should have withstood the task," Thedar said.

Thedar drew me closer and gently pushed my head against his chest. His hand stroked my hair. "Thal," he said, "we all knew that Shaara's love for Shaarvan was woven into the core of her. We knew that from the testing. You let your needs outweigh hers. That is not the Shapechanger way."

There was a moment of silence, and then I heard the sound of Thal weeping. I had never heard a Shapechanger cry. It was like the lonely winds that whistled through a canyon. It was an eerie, frightening sound of desolation.

I pushed away from Thedar. His arms didn't halt me or secure me to him. I could not stand to see Thal as he was. I started to go closer to comfort him, to put my arms about him, and to tell him again that I forgave him, but Spelon's Saberey opened its mouth and gripped my hand in its jaw. The bite didn't hurt me, but I knew he was telling me not to go closer.

"But Thal needs me," I said.

Spelon growled, and his body wedged into me. Thal's sobbing was breaking my heart, but I nodded my compliance. I would not step closer.

"Thal, please. I need your help," I said.

"Shaarvan will help you. My book does not tell me how," he told me. "I cannot undo it."

"Shaarvan will help me, but I need your help, too."

Spelon's huge tiger mouth released me, but apparently, he could communicate with Thedar in his Saberey change because Thedar reached forward, grabbed me, and pulled me back. The Shapechanger cross-over hold secured me against his body then.

"You understand. I had to do it, Thalia."

Okay, no hugging, but I still needed Thal's assistance. I'd have to do that with words only. "Thal, listen to me, please."

"I am Shapechanger, Thalia. Modulate your voice."

"Yes, Thal. I am sorry. Thal, do you know where the potion is that would make me a High Priestess?"

"It would not save you. Shaarvan will save you."

"I know, Thal. But do you know where the potion is?"

"Thedar, Thalia needs a strong hand. You will have to make sure she does not argue. She argues a lot."

Thedar took a single step forward. "Is Shaara a ten?" he asked.

"A ten? I do not know. She would have to light a candle to be a ten. Can you light a candle?" he asked me.

"How do I light it?"

"With your mind, my dear, with your mind."

"Can you teach me how?"

"You are dying. Why would I teach you?"

"Because I need to know."

"Thedar, tell Shaarvan to plant her with another baby. It is the only way to stop her arguments."

"I will tell him, Thal."

I looked up at Thedar. I hoped he would ask Thal the secret of the candle.

"So you think Shaara is a nine?" Thedar asked, ignoring my unspoken request.

"She is definitely a nine, but it is better if she is never tested. Keep her away from the Old Ones."

Thedar pointed at a chair over in the corner. "Thalia, go sit there." He watched as I obeyed, although he didn't need to with Spelon still in Saberey form and guarding me as closely as if he weren't.

"So one needs only to light a candle?" Thedar asked.

Thal laughed. "Think you are clever, huh? What are you going to do — practice? It is not something a male can do. The Power runs in lines, male lines and female lines. That woman over there does not know half the things she can do."

Thal returned to his research, flipping through pages as if we'd already left. I thought he'd forgotten us, but then he turned and looked at me.

"I bet you could do it, woman. The flame is in you. All you have to do is focus, like you do when you are changing shapes. You see the candle lit in your mind and when you open your eyes, it is flaming bright oranges and yellows."

A smile widened Thal's lips. It was not the smile I was used to seeing. It was a strange distortion of the lips, as if they had twisted unevenly in different directions.

"You show me you can do that, Thalia, and I shall give you the potion. Then, Shaarvan cannot have you either."

We left after that. Thal didn't say goodbye. He didn't even look up. He was once more bent over his figures and books about stars.

Spelon growled once, then reverted back. Thedar released me, but Spelon made no effort to reclaim me. Spelon walked beside me, deep in thought.

Thedar was quiet, too, as we walked. Perhaps we were all combing through the information that Thal had so scantily provided. But there was one question I had to ask, the one that frightened me most.

"Thedar, Spelon. Tenor said that a High Priestess has no husband, and Thal said I would lose Shaarvan. Why?"

"A High Priestess is owned by no man."

I stopped and placed my hand on the arm of each male. "But if I wanted to have a husband, could I?"

"That is the point, Shaara. You could have anything you want as High Priestess except a Shapechanger who refuses to bow to you."

"You mean, it is Shaarvan who would refuse me?"

Thedar nodded. "I have known Shaarvan a long time. I have never seen him bow to anyone, but his uncle, and that bow is very stiff."

"You wouldn't obey him," Spelon said.

I ignored that. I'd need to think about it. Instead, I responded to what Thedar had said. "But I wouldn't expect Shaarvan to bow to me."

"What would you want him to do, Shaara?"

"I don't want him to change at all."

Spelon laughed and shook his head. "Careful, Shaara. You know the danger of a lie."

"Thedar?"

"Then you cannot change."

"But I have to do this. The war will go on and on. Thenos could kill Shaarvan or the boys. He could kill all of you — Tevor, Teea, Pathe, and all the other Shapechanger on Altar. Thenos has to be stopped."

"Then, there will be losses."

"Why does it have to be you, Shaara? Why take on this responsibility?" Spelon asked.

"Because I'm the only one who can do it, Spelon. I know I can. I've seen it in my visions."

I turned back to reach inside Thedar, not with Power, but to read the emotions on his face. "But, Thedar," I said, digging deeper. "I don't understand. If I became a High Priestess to kill Thenos, why couldn't I still be Shaarvan's wife?"

Spelon snorted. It sounded so much like his Saberey. I looked over at him to make sure he hadn't Changed again. He hadn't, but he was shaking his head. "Obedience is not something you're good at, Shaara."

That was a fair statement. I shot him a quick smile of agreement.

"Shaara, do you remember when Shaarvan told you that you must thank each of your bondmates for testing you?" Thedar asked.

I nodded. Of course, I remembered that.

"You did not want to obey him. I believe he had to threaten you with the Power then. And, when you refused to marry Thal, Shaarvan had to threaten you with a beating. You have not changed. You constantly rebel. How could you accept the authority of a husband who could no longer enforce his commands?"

"Oh," I said with a very unbrilliant reply. In fact, I had no answer at all. Neither of them seemed to expect one. We walked on.

Shaarvan

I am a traitor to my cause, but I have no choice. I would do no good to Altar as a corpse.

The others do not understand my leaving. There are few of us left who have followed the ways of the Old Ones. The death bond is almost extinct. The Altarians do not understand that Shaara and I will both die if I do not rebuild our bond.

I thank the stars that I still have the Westlan ship. Without it, there would be no hope of saving Shaara. I pray to the Old Ones to watch over her. Only they can keep her alive until I arrive.

I shall reach her in time. I must keep thinking that.

And, then, what shall I do with Shaara? I cannot take her back to Altar with me. Thenos is obsessed with her. But how can I leave her again? How could I find the courage?

Shaara

The Tides keep passing but in slow motion. I had not asked Shaarvan if I could contact him during his flight, and Spelon would not let me. He said that it only increased the odds of Thenos tracking Shaarvan or me.

Spelon bedded down with me each evening. I did not fight him. He held me in his arms and attempted to take care of my Shapechanger needs, but I couldn't sleep beside him. I waited until he fell asleep each night and then unwrapped his arms and paced the night. Nights were lonely and long.

Tren worried over my restlessness. He told me that if I would only close my eyes and think of pleasant things, I would drift off. He didn't understand that it wasn't the abstinence that stole my sleep. Yet, I could not have endured it any other way. I feared that I might kill Spelon if he tried to take me now.

The sustenance that had been keeping me alive was running out. Tren would not tell me how much more there was. But I was down to one meal a day, and my battle lessons with Spelon had been stopped. I was too tired anyway. I did not miss them. It seemed that all I did was rest. At times, I found it exhausting just to watch Shaarac playing or to hold Thandar, and I had to force myself to smile at them. Even smiling seemed fatiguing.

I still practiced with a candle, though. I had placed it beside my bed, and every hour I stared at it. I did what Thal told me to do, but the candle did not light for me. I knew there had to be some trick that Thal had not told me. But I was too tired. I could no longer brood over my failure.

Yesterday, Thedar went and talked with Thal again, but Thal could not remember any secret. I wonder what Tessa would have said. Would she have told me to figure it out, or would she have laughed and joked about males who couldn't remember the simplest things?

Shaarvan

I dream of Shaara each night. She lies in her bed, paler than I remember her. Her cheekbones seem haunted by shadow. Her eyes have lost their shine. But the sight of her is beyond words. She is beautiful.

I do not call out to her. It is better if the link that connects us is not used for communication. I have heard that Thenos is no longer at the palace. It is rumored that he sails the skies in search of Thenosa, the name he has given to Shaara.

Perhaps I shall meet Thenos. I would like to end this war with a battle solely between us. The Stars have foretold of a meeting in space. Yet, the Stars have spoken of a triangle of death. Who is the other vertex? Spelon, Tren, or one of the others?

The Stars do not speak of the victor. The battle has been too evenly matched. "One will die in the triangle, and two will pay the price," I remember it well in the mind of Tessa.

The Stars do not let us see anything clearly. But the prophesy could be soon. Let the death triangle begin. Let it start the moment I have made Shaara well. And, if the one who dies is Thenos, then no price is too high.

Chapter Five

Shaara

Tren has run out of sustenance. He has started injecting me with what he calls sugar water. I no longer care that I am not going to live, except I wanted so badly to see Shaarvan. It seems cruel to have waited all this time for him and never to touch his lips again.

I lie in bed, and my mind drifts. I no longer have the energy to pace, yet still, I cannot sleep. My mind spends its time remembering: golden streaks on hair so soft it is like caressing a cat's fur, a dimpled smile that spreads, lighting up his eyes of gray — a gray as gentle as the morning dew or hard as granite.

His teeth gleam, as white as parched bone in the desert sun, yet laughing and flashing. His smile reminds me of sun-touched leaves flipping in the afternoon breeze. (Although that image makes me smile since his teeth may share the shine of leaves, but certainly not the green.)

I recall his arms, strong as a tiger's jaw, crushing me in an embrace of which I will never complain again. I think about how he thought me brain-damaged after Freinana and then the look in his eyes when he realized I was not.

I smile often these days. How can I not? There is sadness in the air, but I have my recollections. It is almost as if Shaarvan is here.

Tren is picking me up. Why does he disturb me? "Do not take me to the children," I tell him. "I am too tired."

"He is here, Shaara. I am giving you one last injection. There, that is finished. You will be OK now. His ship is touching down. You have made it, my love."

"Shaarvan? Shaarvan is here?"

"I shall take you to him. Spelon gave me permission."

"Shaarvan?"

"He is here. Hold on, my love. Hold on."

I can scarcely believe what Tren has just told me, yet I know he cannot lie to me. Could it possibly be true?

Tren carried me to the control room. They were all there to gather around me. Everyone was smiling. It was a happy moment as we watched Shaarvan's ship join with ours. But, still, I could not believe it. I pinched my arm. Was I awake? Or was this only another one of my daydreams?

In a moment, Shaarvan was there, sweeping me into his arms. My lips clung to his, and my joy was almost painful. My tears started at once, but he did not berate me. His lips seemed to need mine as much as I did. I felt the warmth of him, the specialness. I suddenly knew this was real. Shaarvan had returned!

He did not speak to the others. He carried me to my chamber as we kissed. There were no words spoken between us. I was hungry for them, but I was starved for his body as well. Shaarvan laid me down on the bed and took my dress from me. His clothes soon followed on the floor, and then he was next to me, stroking and weaving the web.

For the first time, I broke free from his lips to speak. "Shaarvan, you do not need to web me. I will never fight you."

"Shaara, my love," he said, between sprinkles of kisses across my face, "I must hurt you to make you mine again. The webs are necessary."

I looked into his eyes, gray as a foggy morning, and I realized then that he was as ill as I was. I took his face in mine, kissed his lips and his cheeks, and said, "Shaarvan, no pain you give me is worse than the separation we have endured. Do what you need to. I will not complain."

His mouth once more descended, and he began the webs again. Every inch of me, he touched and tasted. I was drugged with the feel of him. I whimpered at the agony of the delay.

"Soon, Shaara, soon," he told me.

He took me then, and the ecstasy was just as I'd remembered. The pain came after. It rippled through me in waves. It hurt so much I sought my forest, but Shaarvan would not let me retreat there.

"No, my love, you must feel it, as I do. We share the pain as we share the bond. It is cleansing you of Stegthal's bonds and reclaiming you with mine. It is filling you with my possession. Together, we must experience the bond reforming. And, when the pain is over, we shall once again be one."

"Kiss me, then, Shaarvan. Let us ease the pain with our delight," I said.

Once more, his lips met mine, and the pain faded as our lust built. And when we had once again quenched our need, and the wildness of our passion simmered down, I stroked his chest and face, and I savored the feel of Shaarvan pressed against my body. I breathed in his scent. It was the smell of the sun on the forest trees, the pine needles under our cushioned paws, and Shaarvan. I sighed with happiness.

My hand brushed through his hair. It was more golden now than I had ever seen it as if the sun had melted golden crayons among the tawny brown. It was as soft as I remembered, the fur of a velvet Persian cat. I stroked his arms. The muscles seemed even larger and tighter than before.

I thought of the military drills I'd pulled him away from to talk through the stars. How many pipe weapons had he drilled with over and over? How many boulders had he strained against, lifting and rolling, until they were in position for defense?

His hand lifted up to touch my face. His knuckles, rougher than I remembered, stroked my cheek. I wanted to purr from happiness. He smiled, sharing my thoughts.

I laid my head down on his chest and listened to the sound of his heart beating. "Does it still say, *Shaara, Shaara?*" I asked.

His teeth flashed, and the dimples widened. "No," he said.

I sat up. "What?"

He pulled me down almost roughly, and his arms corralled me tightly. His lips planted kisses up and down my neck, and then he said, "No, my love. It says, *Shaara, Shaara, Shaara*. Three of them in a row. Then it stops and listens and says it again. *Shaara, Shaara, Shaara*. Sometimes, it puts in an extra beat, and it says *forever.*"

"I love you, Shaarvan," I said, and my tears came again.

He sighed at the tears, but he only held me closer, and when I was done, he kissed me again. Then he stood up, swung his legs down to the ground, and began to dress.

I flung myself at him, "Shaarvan, please don't go. I cannot bear to have you out of my sight."

He turned and took my hand. His lips played my palm, and I shivered. He carried me back to the bed, touched his lips to my forehead, and said, "You are half-starved, my poor wife. I wished there had been a way to get more nutrient injections into you. But you will be all right now. I shall go get food for us both. We shall be able to eat now."

"Please, let me go with you. I will be afraid I have dreamed this and that you are not really here," I said.

"I am here, Shaara. I shall leave you only a moment. Do not leave this bed, my wife. That is an order."

"You promise to come back?"

"Yes. I promise."

He was gone for only a short time, but my heart was beating much too quickly as he returned.

I did not want the food he brought. I only wanted Shaarvan's touch. Again, his knuckles stroked my face. "I almost lost you, my soulmate. I shudder to think how close it was."

His voice was so raw with the depth of his feeling, it almost gave way.

He handed me a small piece of bread and ordered me to eat it. I feared the bread would still taste like sawdust and gag me when I tried to swallow it, but the flavor of it, as I chewed, was like heaven. In a moment, I was finished and wanted more.

Shaarvan gave me another small piece and warned me that I would have to wait a while for more. He let me drink a little juice, but even that he limited. I watched him eat his own food, and I felt the pangs of hunger once again.

He laughed, and I froze. I understand in that moment why my laugh hurt Tren so much in the casino. Shaarvan's laugh was like a layer of who Shaarvan was. It was the wrapping paper, all printed up pretty with bows and ribbons. Underneath was the special present, but the laugh held the wrapping of all his love.

As usual, he read my thoughts. "My lovely Shaara, I have so missed the strangeness of your thoughts. I had almost forgotten how to laugh. My sweet little wife, I have not lived without you. It has only been existing."

He bent down and touched his lips to mine and once again laughed. "Wrapping paper?"

Maybe it wasn't wrapping paper. As I listened again, I heard it differently. This time, Shaarvan's laugh was a gypsy's violin playing to my heart.

Thal

Thank the stars! Thalia is going to be all right!

Thedar came by and visited me. He was reserved with me. It felt like a *duty call*, but even so, I appreciated his telling me. It was good to hear the news. I am grateful my little one will not die.

Thedar and Tenor bring me meals and check on my needs from time to time, but whatever friendship we had between us is gone. I have seen Tren only once and Spelon not at all since the day he Shapechanged next to Thalia. Do they not realize that without her I need them more?

I know I deserve their coldness. Yet, if I could undo what I did to Thalia, I would do so in an instant. I wish they realized how ashamed I am.

I feel the huge space between us, the airless pocket of distance. Thedar and Tenor have replaced their friendly pronouns with formal ones. I am aware of it. What can I do to atone? What can I do to change the past?

Little Thalia, I wish on the Somber Tree that I had not used my fist on you. If only you had not been so rebellious that day . . . If you had accepted my new bond. Why did you not see that it was my right? You were mine, but you would not own to it. What else could I have done?

Shaarvan will be angry with me. Perhaps he will kill me. I welcome my Passing. I will tell him that I owned Thalia. I took his bond away, and I owned her for that one ride. I soared through the blackness of the sky and achieved the light. Let him kill me. She was mine.

Shaara

Tren knocked at our door, and Shaarvan welcomed him in. Tren had brought us more food, even though we had not yet eaten all the bread Shaarvan had gotten for us.

Tren put down the tray and stood there nervously. His eyes were trying not to look at me as I lay there beneath the covers with my dress still on the floor.

Shaarvan rose up to greet him. "Thank you, my brother, for what you did for Shaara."

"I wish I had stored more sustenance. I gave all that we had to her, but she ran out four days ago. Will she be OK?"

"She will be fine now. I have mended the tear. But, perhaps we should keep her on the sustenance for a while."

"No food?" I cried out.

"Perhaps I shall withhold it to use as training. You have forgotten again how to be a Shapechanger wife."

I gasped. Shaarvan turned around to look at me. "Ah, Shaara, I am sorry. You are not up to my teasing yet." He came to me and pressed his lips to my forehead. "I shall leave Tren with you, my love. I shall bring all the sustenance that I have on my ship."

He turned to Tren. "You will stay with her? She may have another piece of bread, but no more even if she begs."

Shaarvan started to leave, but he turned back once more to look at Tren. "You project almost as much as Shaara." It was a warning. I felt Tren go rigid.

"It is all right to love her, Tren, but you must trust me to know what is best for my wife." For a moment, the two were locked in a battle. I could feel the Power that flared between them, but it was over almost as soon as it had begun, and Tren looked away.

"I have never come between you two," Tren said in a voice that spoke more of fatigue than defeat.

"Stay with her, Tren. I trust you. If Shaara eats too much at once in her starved condition, she will vomit it up. That is the only reason I limit her."

The door slid closed, and Tren sat down in the chair.

"Tren." I hated to bother him. He was staring at his boots like they had worms crawling on them.

He looked up at me, and his face turned red.

"Tren, could you please give me the bread now?" I knew I should have been more sympathetic, but Tren had seen me nude before, and I was covered up with a blanket. Besides, I was starving.

He handed the bread to me without a word. I reached up, and his eyes traveled my body beneath the blanket.

I sighed, but I started chewing.

"You are happy now?" he asked me.

"Stars! I am so happy I could burst."

"Then you will let him take care of you?"

I started to agree, but I realized that Tren meant something different. "I am still practicing on the candle. It will not yet light for me."

"Good."

"Tren, I need to light it."

"Perhaps it did not work while you were ill. Maybe when you are well, it will flame up."

"That's it! Tren, of course, that's it! How could I have been so stupid?"

I looked over at the candle and focused again. I shut my eyes and thought about the light that I would see when I opened them. I painted it in my mind: red in the center, gold and yellow, with streaks of white. When I opened my eyes, I was sure I would see it lit, but the wick was still black and burned from past lighting. It held no flame.

When I looked over at Tren, I thought he would have seen my failure, but his eyes were once again glued to my body.

"Tren, stop it."

His eyes held the same haunted look as Thal's.

"Tren, you have seen my body. Why do you stare now? I am so thin I cannot hold your interest."

"I am sorry, Shaara. I should not be here, seeing you in your bed."

"I saw you in yours," I said, and the reminder of his naked body as I had seen him plunging into the casino girl sent a ripple of desire through my body for Shaarvan's hard, sinewy frame.

The door slid open, and I almost flung myself across the room at him, but Tren was there, and I lay still. My eyes bathed Shaarvan with kisses. Shaarvan came to my side at once and kissed my lips. We almost forgot Tren in our need. Tren rose to go, and Shaarvan reluctantly pulled away.

"Tren, I am sorry," Shaarvan said. "It is the bonding madness that flares between us now." Shaarvan's eyes did not leave my face as he spoke, yet he continued. "I would see my son. Would you do another kindness and bring him to me?"

Shaarvan recycled my dress and tossed me a clean one. I put it on, grateful to be clothed if people were going to be coming in and out of my room. But, as I pulled it over my head, I was thinking about Shaarac meeting Shaarvan. I didn't even feel the needle as Shaarvan injected the nutrient into me. I knew Shaarvan's anger, and I was frightened of it.

His gray eyes settled on me, and he read my fear. "What is it? Answer, Shaara. I shall hear it now."

"Shaarvan, Thal commanded that Shaarac be called Thaarac. Shaarac does not know his rightful name."

"And you fear I shall be angry with you?"

"There is more, my husband. Thal called himself Shaarac's father. I was a coward for not insisting that Shaarac be taught the truth."

"You have never been a coward, Shaara. You only obeyed your husband's will. You have nothing to fear. Only what you do willfully brings my anger."

199

I tried not to think of what I was planning to do. I knew it would come under his definition of willful.

The door slid open, and a little voice cried out, "Mommy, Mommy!" Shaarac ran to me and threw his arms around me. Slurpy kisses attacked my face, but they were a welcome joy. I hugged him and kissed him back.

Shaarac put up with it for longer than usual, and then he pulled back to ask, "Mommy, not sick anymore?"

"I'm not sick anymore. I feel wonderful, better than in a long, long time!"

"Shaarac, come here," Shaarvan ordered.

Shaarac turned to look at the stranger. His eyes grew dark. Shaarac's eyes were still more of a blue than a gray, but when he was angry, he looked Shapechanger. "My name is Thaarac," he declared. His little body drew itself up proudly. He was so very like Shaarvan. I smiled.

I turned to share my smile with Shaarvan, but he was not smiling.

"Come here, my son."

Shaarac would not disobey a Shapechanger, even one he'd never seen before, but his eyes grew grim at the words *my son*.

"You have grown tall since I last saw you. Has your mother told you of your birth?"

"She not s'posed to," he lisped.

"I see."

"You not s'posed to be here. Mommy is Thal's."

I watched the battle in Shaarac's little mind. He knew somehow that this male was a threat to everything he'd known.

"Your mommy is only a woman, and she must obey her owner. I am her owner," Shaarvan told his son. Shaarvan's eyes were as serious as if he spoke with an adult. "Thal took care of your mommy for me. I had to go away, but I have come back. Now, your mommy is mine again."

"Zat true, Mommy?"

I nodded, but Shaarvan said, "I am Shapechanger. You know it is true."

Shaarac flushed and looked down at his shoes.

"Shaarac," Shaarvan said, "I shall tell you of your birth."

"Can I sit with Mommy?"

"Yes, we shall all sit with your mommy."

The three of us snuggled down under the covers. Shaarac curled up close to me, and his father sat on the other side of him.

There are moments that we treasure in our life. We do not choose them consciously, but somewhere inside us, a hand reaches out and cups the memory like a jewel to be held within our hearts forever. I love my husband, and the times that we joined in the days that followed were pleasures of unbelievable heights, but it is always the pearls of other moments I cherish most.

With Shaarvan, my beloved, in the bed beside me and Shaarac in between us, every word of that precious time that followed is etched inside my store of memories. It is the diamond of my jewels. I take it out often now that I am once again without my love.

But, how easily it all flowed then. Shaarvan began his story with his son. "I planted the seed in your mommy here." He placed his hand across Shaarac and touched my stomach.

Shaarac giggled. "I know. Daddy telled me."

"I planted the seed in Mommy that grew to be you. You were very, very tiny then, but you grew big."

"Like Thandar. I growed big like Thandar. Mommy got fat!" His arms showed Shaarvan how big I had become, but I did not think I was ever as big as Shaarac remembered.

"You kicked Mommy lots inside her. I felt you kick."

"Thandar kicked Mommy." Shaarac nodded, like he and Shaarvan were two adults comparing stories.

"Then one day, you kicked Mommy so hard she knew you wanted to come out."

"Thandar, too."

"Mommy was eager for you to be born, and so was I because we knew we would love you very much."

"Males not say love." Shaarac shook his head. He looked just like Spelon when he said it.

Shaarvan looked at me when he continued. "I think that is wrong, Shaarac. We males use other words. We say that we give our hearts, but your mommy has taught me that it is the same."

"Spel say . . . "

"Spel? Oh, Spelon." Shaarvan laughed. "Spelon is your friend, Shaarac?" He watched as Shaarac nodded emphatically. "He is my friend, too, but I was telling you a story. Mommy and I watched you being born. It was a happy time."

"Where is my daddy?" Shaarac demanded. He was getting worried.

"Your mommy did not know Thal then. Thal was not there."

"Daddy plants seed."

"That is right. Will you show me your brother? Thal planted Thandar's seed as I planted yours. I would like to know Thandar, too."

It was perfectly done. Shaarvan was magic. I kissed his lips.

"Mommy!" came the indignant cry of my son.

"Remember, Shaarac, she is a woman. She must do as she is told."

"I know," he said, but his thumb found its way to his mouth and stayed there. He had not done that for a long time, but I said nothing.

"Will you let me go with you?" I asked.

For a moment, I thought Shaarvan would say *no*, but he nodded. "I shall carry you."

In Shaarvan's arms, with Shaarac dragging us to see his brother, it was impossible to imagine the flow of love between us would not continue as it was. Perhaps Barquel found me once more and evened out the good and bad, or maybe it was the Wheel of Change. I'd lost track of time. Thal would have said it was a star building to a nova. I suppose they are all the same. Happiness is fleeting.

But I have jumped forward in my story, and I must stop and go back.

When we reached the nursery, Thedar was there with Thandar. Shaarvan put me down in the chair and took the baby from Thedar. He thanked Thedar for all he had done for us, and then Shaarvan looked down at the baby he held. His eyes were gentle and loving as if Thandar were his.

"You are a fine little one," Shaarvan said. "I bet you grow to be as tall as my big son, Shaarac."

Shaarac joined his father. They sat down on the floor and talked about Thandar and the ship and about life.

Thandar had never met a stranger, yet he accepted Shaarvan right from the start. His eyes twinkled, and he made his baby noises. He drooled all over Shaarac and Shaarvan, and the three of them laughed.

If only Thandar were Shaarvan's, I thought. Then, I could love him too. How happy we could be as a family in the little wolf's lair of a cottage that Shaarvan owned.

"I am pleased you have given me two fine sons, Shaara, and we shall one day live on Altar as a family, but the wolf's lair is gone. Thenos burned it. I am sorry."

"No," I cried out. "Not our beautiful cottage."

"It was only pieces of wood, Shaara. It was too small for us anyway. We shall build a bigger house someday."

"The forest? Did he hurt the forest?"

"No, the forest is still there, my love. I shall take you when it is safe."

Shaarvan stood up and asked, "Which of my sons will you hold, wife? I shall play catch with the other one."

"With me, with me! Mommy, hold Thandar, OK?"

I smiled. In one swoop, Shaarvan had forced me to hold Thandar and had received his son's acceptance. Did he always get his way?"

"Always," Shaarvan whispered in my ear as he handed me the baby.

Thandar grabbed at my hair. His eyes laughed at the feel of it. I remembered when Shaarac had done the same thing. I held his little hand. It was so small. Shaarac's had been just the same size at a thirtyTide. They were so alike, these two little Shapechanger boys.

Thandar's chubby little cheeks smiled happily. He was such a good little baby. I missed the feel of him at my breast. Both boys had been robbed far too early of their breast milk. I hoped it would not harm them.

I looked up to see Shaarac trying to catch the pillow that Shaarvan had tossed. It fell not two feet from his stubby little toddler hands. He laughed when Shaarvan scooped it up and tossed it back.

"Oog," Thandar said, watching them. I knew he wasn't old enough to talk yet, but it was a sound he seemed to like. His eyes studied me. "Oog," he told me seriously, and then he laughed. His eyes were already turning Shapechanger-gray. They were grayer already than Shaarac's.

He grabbed my arm and rocked himself up and down. For a moment, he sat still and watched Shaarvan and Shaarac play toss. Then again, his eyes moved back to me. His little button nose crinkled up, and his lips spread wide.

"Ooth," he declared, and I had to laugh.

Then he started laughing. "Ooth, ooth, ooth!"

I looked up to see Shaarvan coming towards me. Shaarac was perched on his father's shoulders. My son's little, chubby toddler legs were wrapped around Shaarvan's neck. Shaarac's hands clung to Shaarvan's pelt of hair.

"My new daddy play catch," Shaarac said. Thandar smiled happily. "Oog!" he bubbled. Shaarvan smiled at us all. His eyes met mine, and he held them. "Our sons are happy children. They must feel the abundance of our love."

There was meaning in his words, and I felt it. It wasn't a warning exactly, but there was a sour note in the melody, and I knew the fault was mine.

We took the children with us to the control room in search of Thedar. He was the one who was supposed to be on babysitting duty for the day. The others were not there, and Thedar was playing cards, looking thoroughly bored. He jumped up when he saw us, and a smile lit his face.

"Shaara, you are better?"

I nodded, but I was tired, even from so short a walk. I sat down beside him and played two of his cards.

He growled at me and pretended to swat my hand. "Your wife has an irritating habit of being a sharp card player. If Thal had let her keep the winnings, we would all be poor!"

Then he realized what he'd said. "I am sorry, Shaarvan. Should I have mentioned . . . ?"

"Thal took care of Shaara for a long time. I am glad he did not allow Shaara to rob you of your wealth." Shaarvan's eyes were laughing when he finished.

"Thedar, perhaps Shaarac could show you how well he plays catch."

"I would like that very much. Would you show me, Shaarac?"

Shaarac nodded and was attempting to pull him away when Thedar asked, "Would you like me to take Thandar back, too, now?"

"No, thank you, Thedar. My wife and I have some things to discuss about Thandar."

Shaarvan waited for Thedar and Shaarac to leave, and then he turned to me. "I am afraid we have a problem with this little guy."

"A problem?"

"It is too bad. He is a cute little fellow."

"Shaarvan, what do you mean?"

"Shaara, I know you understand. He complicates things."

"What do you mean, he complicates things?"

I was watching Shaarvan bounce Thandar on his knee. The baby was giggling away.

"Thal cannot keep him. Tenor told me about Thal when I went to get your sustenance. He is in no condition to take care of his son. And we cannot keep him. You have no love for him."

Shaarvan stopped juggling Thandar. The baby reached out and tugged at Shaarvan's shirt. The baby was happy, but Shaarvan was looking gloomy.

"My bondmates adore Thandar," I told Shaarvan.

"No, without a mother, Thandar is not going to make it, Shaara. The best thing we can do for him is to get Spelon to . . ." Shaarvan used the sign that meant "end it."

I sprang up off my seat. "Shaarvan, you don't mean you'd order Spelon to kill Thandar?"

He didn't answer me. His eyes just watched me. I grabbed Thandar off Shaarvan's knee and held the baby close. "I won't let you."

"Shaara, a clean death is always better than neglect."

"No, Shaarvan. Please, don't do this." I kissed Thandar's precious little head with all its baby curls. "Please, please don't hurt him."

Thandar was delighted with all the attention. He gurgled happily. "Ogugla!" he told me.

"Shaarvan, please." The tears were falling down my cheeks now, but I ignored them. Thandar caught my hair and placed a strand in his mouth. "Shaarvan, don't you understand? I love Thandar."

"Good."

I froze. "What do you mean *good*?"

"It means I am glad you realize that you love him. Now come here."

"No, not unless you . . ."

"Obey." The command came with all the history of Shaarvan's training. I could no sooner have disobeyed his command than . . . My feet were taking me to him before I had the chance to think.

"Give me my son."

Shaarvan was running hot and cold. Now Thandar was his son again? He took the baby before I could pull back. Again, he placed Thandar on his knee and juggled him up and down.

"Shaarvan, what are you going to do?"

"Shaara, Shapechanger do not kill babies."

"Then why did you say . . .? You made me think . . ."

"Thandar needs your love, Shaara. He does not understand about war and separation or who his father was."

"You will accept him as yours?"

"You gave birth to two sons, Shaara. I shall acknowledge both. Thal and I shall share the fatherhood of this one."

"I love you, Shaarvan," I said, kissing his cheek, "but that was a cruel trick you played on me."

"It was effective."

"But cruel."

"Ah, wife, you are still difficult."

"I know. My lord has told me so many times."

"I left Altar for you. My honor, my parents, my military command, they all await my return, and now I have to figure out what is best to do with you."

"Shaarvan, it is always best to keep me at your side. I can control my projections now. I have been practicing other things, too, so I can join you. I can load a short pipe and a long one. I can shoot it, too, if Altar will allow that. And Spelon has taught me about knives and where to use them to cause the most damage.

I can read almost anyone's mind, except a Warlord's, and I can still my projections or shoot them further than the distance of the ship. I can do a little of Spelon's kick fighting, and once I fatten up again, you will see that my body is tough and strong. I will be able to march at your side. I can be quiet now, and I promise I will learn anything you need me to know . . ."

Shaarvan watched me as he listened. He did not seem angry that I could do these things, only amused. "I suppose you talked your bondmates into teaching you all that?"

I nodded.

Shaarvan's finger toyed with my hair for a moment as he thought. "Who put the welts on your body . . . Thal?"

"Spelon."

"Why?"

I sighed. Suddenly, my campaign wasn't going well. When I told Shaarvan the truth, he would think I was still argumentative. He would not want to take me with him.

I sighed. There was no way I could keep the truth from Shaarvan. He would unwrap me like an onion if I didn't confess openly. "Spelon said I was Thal's by law because you had been gone for so long. I lost my temper and called him a worm."

"A worm, Shaara? You are lucky five welts are all he gave you, my foolish one."

Shaarvan was shaking his head like he couldn't believe even I could be that stupid. My eyes fell to the floor.

"Why was it Spelon who did the punishing of you?"

"Thal gave me to Spelon for the day and night so he could have his revenge."

"I felt his bond on you. It was deeper than I had allowed it. Did he take you, Shaara? "

"No."

"I am glad. The riding of a Shapechanger woman should never be a punishment."

"But that's what made Thal so angry, that and the fact that I did not feel any of the punishment. I just went away to the forest, and it sheltered me until Spelon was finished. Thal said I was at least a nine now."

"Nine? Shaara, a ten, is what Tessa is. You must be mistaken."

I shrugged. I would not argue with Shaarvan over that.

"You can Shapechange at will?"

"Even to change my face and body. Thal trained me."

Shaarvan's hand was stroking my face. I knew he wasn't interested in sex, but his touch sent ripples of desire through me.

"Was Thal a good husband . . . before?"

I sighed. The last thing I wanted to talk about was Thal, but I knew I had to answer. "He tried, Shaarvan. He just wasn't you."

That developed into a long, deep kiss. It was later that I realized Shaarvan had not told me what he would do with me.

Shaarvan

I left her sleeping soundly. But before I slipped away, I stood and stared down at her. Her hair wreathed her face. It was darker than before as if her illness had taken away its golden highlights. I felt an urge to cradle her in my arms; she was so precious to me. How fragile she had become.

I steeled myself to walk away. She needed rest. It would restore her strength. But what was I going to do with her after she recovered?

I could not help the smile that broke out when I thought back over the things she had said. So she could march by my side and wrestle with our enemy. I had to laugh at that. If she only knew how absurd that seemed when her tiny body seemed only a whisper of what it had been before.

I imagined that the others had merely given her encouragement to try to keep her alive. Shaara was no more a fighter than she was a level nine.

But what should I do with her? Spelon had shown that he was worthy of her guardianship, but to hand her over to another so soon . . . could she bear that?

She was Shapechanger. She would do as I told her, but could I endure another's arms about her? Could I stand to leave her behind again?

Shaara

I woke and discovered that I was alone. The bed felt like an anthill. I left it and showered. I was thrilled to put on the forest greens of Altar once again, but I chose a thicker material than was in vogue there. I was embarrassed at how skinny I had gotten.

I thumbed the door cautiously. I didn't know if Shaarvan had locked me in, and I was afraid of the shock that sometimes accompanied his doors. But he had not turned on the force field.

I found the others sitting at the table, discussing the war. I was unsure if I was welcome. Shaarvan rose up to greet me and met me with a kiss.

"How do you feel, my love?" he asked.

My face heated, but I also smiled. Didn't he know that with him there, I could have danced or flown? I felt that good!

I hadn't answered him, but instead of becoming angry, he laughed softly and led me over to the table. He sat me down on the bench beside him and pushed his plate in front of me. A hunk of bread and some grape-like fruits lay on it. I popped one into my mouth.

Thedar brought me a drink, and I thanked him. Shaarvan glanced at me and then at Thedar, but he didn't stop his story.

"The second moon of Altar, Clofa, we called it, contained only the elders. There were no training facilities or laboratories like Chroma, the other moon, has. There were no people on Clofa who even contested Thenos' reign. It was a senseless murder."

I remembered the hamster cage-looking dwellings I'd seen on Clofa when Shaarvan had first brought me to Altar. The thought of all those people dying made me teary-eyed.

Why did Thenos destroy their settlement? There had to be a reason for it. Why?

The males had already moved on to a discussion of Thenos. It seemed like he had unlimited Power. How was he achieving that? What drug was amplifying it?

"Shaarvan, were there any Shapechanger on Clofa? Were any of them Old Ones?"

I felt Shaarvan's anger before he spoke. What had I done wrong?

"This is a Council of Lords, Shaara. I shall allow you to remain only if you are silent."

For a moment, I wanted to stand up and march away. I was that irritated with Shaarvan's unfairness. But I took in a deep breath and dropped my eyes. I was not going to allow my reaction to his injustice to sabotage my return to Altar. Nor did I want to be excluded from hearing the males' discussions.

Shaarvan nodded, pleased by my acceptance.

"Well done," Spelon said, but I did not know who he was praising.

Out of the corner of my eye, I saw Tren raise his eyebrow at me, probably mocking my subservience.

The males' discussion continued, and I felt Thedar's eyes on me. I looked up, but he didn't seem to be focusing on me. His eyes were thoughtful but distant.

"It is strange that Shaara asked that question," Thedar said. "I also puzzle over why Thenos destroyed that settlement. Is he so mad that he strikes without reason?"

"He is mad, Thedar, but his madness usually harbors genius. We have analyzed the data of that hit and have found only Parthrol. He was the one who sponsored Thenos on Westla. He was Shapechanger, but not an Old One, nor of their lineage. He was also senile. It is hard to believe he could have been a threat to Thenos."

"Thal would know," I said before I thought.

Shaarvan flashed the *leave sign* at me. I looked into his eyes. They told me nothing. It didn't matter. I knew I had displeased him. I stood up to go.

"She is right, you know," Tren said.

Everyone froze.

"Shaara has insights we do not have. Perhaps she should be allowed to speak? We could always ignore the trivia."

Tren was gambling. He had interfered with Shaarvan's rights. Tren would lose face with the others if Shaarvan took affront to it.

Shaarvan flashed a *hold* at me. His eyes traveled the group. "So Shaara has achieved wisdom, or is it that you are all besotted with her?"

No one spoke. I kept my head down. I knew that Shaarvan would not wish to dishonor his brother but to allow a woman to speak in a Council of Lords? How much would Shaarvan bend?

"Tren has presented an interesting proposition. I shall ask my question in another way," Shaarvan said. "My friends, what is your opinion on this matter?"

Spelon stood up. Of course, I knew what he would say. He'd want me confined to the role of a submissive and subservient female.

"I agree with Tren," Spelon said. "Shaara has shown that her mind is as keen as many a male's. She has set her feet on the path of the warrior. I move she stay and be allowed to speak."

I was incredulous.

Thedar stood up. "I agree. Shaara is too young for wisdom, but from the mouth of an innocent flows a new way of thinking."

Tenor rose. "I do not believe that the choice is ours, Shaarvan. If Shaara were mine, I would urge her to speak, but she is not mine. We all know that Shaara's greatest fault is her strong will. As her husband, you must choose whether her training is more important than the accidental flow of wisdom she may offer us."

Shaarvan turned me to face him. He raised my chin and stared into my eyes. "When I left, you were only a child, but even then, there was the light of intelligence in your eyes."

He looked around at the males sitting at the table. "Teea, my mother, now sits on the Council of Elders in Altar. She has been instrumental in the war against Thenos. She has even begun to carry a short pipe. Change, it seems, is all about us."

Once more, he turned and looked at me. "It is a narrow and treacherous path, Shaara. Can you walk it without injury?"

I did not understand, but I would do as Shaarvan wished. I bowed my head.

Shaarvan nodded. "Walk it gently, my wife." He motioned me to sit and then turned to Tren. "Bring Thal to us. We shall see if there is any merit to Shaara's words."

It was all a gamble. What if Thal's mind still wandered? What if he knew nothing about Clofa?"

I thought that Shaarvan was listening to something Thedar was saying, but his knuckles brushed against my cheek. I relaxed then. Shaarvan was not displeased with me. Yet, was it not shallow of me to fret over Shaarvan's pleasure?

"It is because you are centered on the Primary that I allowed you to stay, Shaara."

I sighed and accepted.

Thal's entrance was hesitant. His eyes glanced briefly at Shaarvan and flitted away. Then he saw me and smiled.

"Ah, Shaara. The bloom of the circa is in your cheeks. I do not need to ask if you are well again."

"Thal, my friend," Shaarvan began. "You honored me by taking care of my wife for longer than either of us had foreseen. But I have to ask you. What made you think you could bond Shaara tighter than I had allowed?"

"You told me it could not be done, Shaarvan. You did not tell me why. I found the solution to the how, but I did not know its effect on Shaara. I am sorry I betrayed your trust."

Shaarvan sighed and gazed at me. "Perhaps it was meant to be." For a moment, he looked out through the screen that showed our passage through the stars. Again, he sighed. "Tessa once said the pathway of change is written in the history of the future."

"Ah, the ripples of the future hold the tiny droplets of change," Thal said, "I remember. It is like the stars — which ones do we choose to visit, knowing that our choice creates the history of our future."

For a moment, we all looked outwards, watching the ship's passage through the darkness of space.

Shaarvan's voice brought us back. "There is another matter between us, Thal. I was not pleased to hear you handed Shaara to Spelon when he was in full warrior rage."

"I had already beaten Thalia once for her rudeness to Spelon. It only halted her disrespect for a short while. When she erupted at Spelon that day, I made the decision that he would have to be the one to teach her the penalty."

"Unchaperoned?"

"You made him Third. Would he have been chaperoned if I were dead?"

"He would have owned Shaara, then. That is the difference. In his rage, Spelon could have killed Shaara. If he had done so, despite our friendship, I would have ripped you like a man."

Tenor and Thedar bolted up, ready to break apart the battle they were anticipating. Spelon also leaped up, but his motion was towards me. He jerked me backward, away from the two males.

Thal did not react to Shaarvan's insult. He said simply, "Had Spelon injured her, I would have deserved your punishment."

"Why did you risk her?" Shaarvan said, his shadowed fur growing more prominent.

"There are many things you do not know about your wife, Shaarvan."

I tried to wiggle out of Spelon's arm hold, but he held me tightly. "I have to stop this," I whispered to him.

"You were warned once by Thal. Have you forgotten?"

I remembered. I could not come between two warriors. Spelon was right. I stopped fighting him.

"My wife is half-starved. Other than that, I see little change, Thal."

"You are blind. You have not looked hard enough, then. I did not fear that Spelon would hurt Shaara badly because she has the Power. Already, she has more projection than Tessa. Did you ever hear of Trepa? Trepa took on Tem when he was young. From all accounts, she almost beat him."

Spelon snorted contemptuously. It drew the eyes of both Thal and Shaarvan.

"Let Shaara go, Spelon. There will be no violence here."

Gratefully, I dropped onto the bench, as did the others. Spelon sat down beside me and seized my wrist. Tren glared at him for doing so, but Spelon ignored it.

"Trepa would have conquered Tem, but he offered her something she wanted even more. Shall I say, to shelter Shaara, something she *desired?*"

Again, Shaarvan tensed. Thal had insulted Tem, even though the story must be true, or Thal would not have told it.

Thal continued, ignoring Shaarvan's fiercely glowing eyes. "Trepa and Shaara would be evenly matched, I think. Shaara would have no need to give in for what Trepa . . ."

"Enough. This fantasy is a waste of time," Shaarvan said, cutting Thal off.

"Hardly that, Shaarvan. It is the path of the stars, the history of our future. You see, we both want Shaara, but she belongs to no male. Not now."

Spelon's arm seized me in the crosshold. Once again, he expected trouble.

"Ah, Spelon," said Thal. "You still protect her. She does not need your protection now. When she lights the candle, the nova will begin, and Shaara will be a new High Priestess.

"It is the attributes, Shaara," Thal said suddenly. "You are not focusing enough on the attributes."

I have seen Shaarvan clear his mind of all the clutter so he could focus on one thing. He did it then. All the jumble that had been thrown at him to process, he sent back to storage for later. He drew himself up, and as if none of this battle of words had risen between them, he said, "Thal, tell us about Parthrol and Thenos."

Thal was as surprised as the others. I felt their emotions in the same way I felt Thandar in the nursery at that moment. Thandar wanted his bottle. I soothed him and sent him back to sleep. It would hold him for a while. I could not bear to leave, not yet.

I had broken Shaarvan's concentration. He turned and stared at me. He had felt what I'd done. It was another piece of information he would store for later processing. He turned back to listen to Thal.

"Parthrol and Thenos? Why, Parthrol was the one who taught Thenos about the Old Ones. I knew Parthrol well. Unfortunately, he was not really popular. He came up with a drug to increase the Power of a Shapechanger, kind of like the vial Shaara will drink soon, except Parthrol wanted to increase the Power of males.

"There was a rumor that he tried it on a young Shapechanger, and the boy went mad. It supposedly broke all the imprinting. The boy began to — how should I say it? — not use women to deal with his sexual tensions — and he was able to brazenly lie without any illness. Of course, as I said, it was only the kind of talk that goes from mouth to mouth in whispers."

"Who else knew about the drug?"

"I am certain Thenos did. Do you think that is how he became Powerful enough to follow Shaara?"

"Tell me about that," Shaarvan demanded.

"She woke up screaming. I can tell you that. She said that Thenos looked like you, but she knew the difference."

"Shaara, what can you add?" Shaarvan asked me.

I met Shaarvan's eyes. "It was strange how Thenos found me, but he always kept asking me where I was. And he knew when I was seeded with Thandar, but not whose seed was in me."

"So Thenos feels you but cannot locate you?"

"I don't know. We always left when he contacted me."

"Shaara, can you contact him?"

"Please don't make me do that."

"Can you?"

"I don't know. Maybe."

"Did you know that Thenos probably bonded Thalia?" Thal asked.

"I guarded them," Shaarvan said. "It is not possible." Shaarvan was glaring at me.

"Shaara told me that one-time Thenos kissed her hand — the day before you left Altar. She said he hurt her."

"Thenos apologized to her, but . . . perhaps it is possible. Shaara, see if you can contact him. If you two are bonded . . . I want you to try, hold it only a moment, then cut if off. We shall all help you if you need us."

"You ask me to live my nightmares? Why? How will it help?"

I half expected Shaarvan to signal *Do not argue* or to snap at me to *obey*, but he walked towards me. Spelon moved away without a word, and Shaarvan drew me up and turned me around to face him.

"Perhaps it will not, Shaara. But, if you can touch his mind and locate him, it may help Altar."

I reached up, placed my hand on Shaarvan's face then nodded. He knew I could not refuse him. I looked at the others. All of them were watching me. I closed my eyes and thought of Thenos, Thenos making puppy dog eyes, Thenos laughing with me, rolling on the floor, Thenos as he looked at Shaarac that first time. *"Thenos, where are you, my brother?*

Chapter Six

Shaara

It was not a comet that took me to him. Crimson Black, galloping through the solar particles, took me there. Thenos was on a ship, not as far away as I'd imagined, but close, very close.

"Thenos. You have called me. What do you want?"

"Shaara, you came. You came to me on your own."

"Why did you want me to come to you those times? The others would not let me. They said you would hurt me. Would you, Thenos?"

"Shaara, you are mine. I do not want to hurt you. I want to be with you. Do you understand?"

"No."

"You are still innocent. I like that, Shaara. I shall teach you much."

"Where are you?"

"I am coming for you, my little sister. Be ready."

"Shaara, wake up. Wake up, my soul."

I opened my eyes and found that Shaarvan had laid me down on the floor. He was kneeling there beside me with my hand at his lips.

"I am sorry, my love," he said. "I should not have asked you to do it. It was too hard for you."

"It wasn't hard, Shaarvan. But Thenos is broken inside, like Thal. He is coming for me on a ship. He is very close. I rode Crimson Black to him, and it was not far."

"Tenor, turn on the discoverers. Thedar, Thal, determine what weapons we have. My ship has almost none. Tren, pray to your gods. And you, my treasure . . . Wait, Tren, save your prayers. You had better go to the boys and feed Thandar. I am putting Shaara back to bed. She is still weak."

Shaarvan left me in my room alone. It was what I needed. The candle and I had business with each other.

I built the colors up — the reds, the orange, the gold, and the yellow. I knew the appearance. I had constructed it so many times in my mind. I could do that almost instantly now. Small at the bottom — a wisp of smoke first, then taper the wick, building upwards and outwards.

Hotter, hotter, until it burst with an urge to burn so uncontrollably that it bloomed. Then, the leaping of the scorchingly hot flame, upwards, outwards. The head was next. Hot air rising at the top, fanning out — the force of it, the Power as I lowered towards the center — the jeweled center — red like a ruby stone glowing externally in pure energy. I breathed the strength of it out of my mouth, knowing the feel, the warmth, the desirable flaming, and the intensity. It was my inner flame, my essence, my ecstasy. It felt wonderful!

I did not need to open my eyes. I knew I had done it. The candle, flickering in the deep calm of the room, was me. The depths and heights, the warmth and the flame of the heat — it was my soul, joyfully burning the wick of life.

Thal reached me first, although they all had felt it. Thal had the potion. He handed it to me.

Shaarvan entered the room next. He looked at the candle and then at me. "No, Shaara. I forbid it," he said.

The others crowded around. Would they be on Shaarvan's side or on mine?

For a moment, I thought about not drinking whatever was in the bottle. It wouldn't make a difference — except to them. There was no magic in the bottle Thal had handed to me. I had passed the test. I was already High Priestess.

"Shaara, do not do this. I shall not permit you to be High Priestess," Shaarvan said, taking a step closer. The others stopped him. So much would they help my cause.

"Shaarvan, I must kill Thenos. Our ship is nearly weaponless, as are you."

"I forbid it. You are my wife. You will obey me."

"The Shapechanger command. What Power it had once held over me. I used to quiver from its force. But it held no strength against me now. I was unstoppable.

"I'm sorry, Shaarvan. I shall always love you." I drank the liquid.

The males needed a show to convince them of the difference. I understood that instinctively. How strange that women understood the male so perfectly while males never attempted to comprehend us at all.

I gasped and held my sides. I screamed as if the pain were rending. I fell to the floor, moaning and projecting great waves of agony.

Shaarvan sprang forward. He held me in his arms. I could barely hold onto my image of great suffering because I ached so for his lips.

"Please, kiss me," I cried. "I'm sorry, Shaarvan."

His lips joined mine, but the kiss was not satisfying. There was no depth. He had turned away from me already. He picked me up and laid me on the bed. Then he turned and walked away.

One by one, the other males filtered out. First Tenor, then Thal, then Thedar. Then, only Tren and Spelon were left.

"I need the short pipe, Spelon. And I'll need you to keep Shaarvan away while I deal with Thenos. I will only get one chance. Do you trust me?"

"You are a warrior, Shaara. I trust you. I shall bring the pipe, and later, I shall keep Shaarvan away."

Spelon left, and then there was only Tren. "The babies?" I asked.

"I gave them something to make them sleep."

He was smiling a mockery of a smile. I'd been aware of his disbelief throughout my act. Yet, he had not warned the others. He had stayed true to me. "You are the only one who saw through my projections, Tren. Why is that so?"

"Why did you project a lie?" he countered.

"I was already High Priestess, but the others would not have accepted me without the myth."

"But, if you had not drunk the potion, you could have kept Shaarvan."

"No. Shaarvan does not want a High Priestess for a wife. He cannot tolerate the idea. It was not my disobedience that turned him away. It was the fact that his pride was wounded. The pride of a male is the source of his Power. If Shaarvan did not turn from me, he would have lost that Power. Only when he regains his pride will he desire me again."

"You could let him go so easily?"

"How can you ask that? The pain of the potion was real in that it was my knowledge of Shaarvan's desertion. That was what I projected. It was not all an act, Tren."

"There was more to the lighting of that candle, I think. You are changed."

I sighed. Tren was my best friend, but I could not reveal the enlightenment of the candle to him. Yet, I would tell him more than the others.

I nodded. "That is true, Tren. I will never be the same, but every event in one's life changes one. It is only that some alterations leave more visible changes. And sometimes, the changes are observable only in the way that people view one.

"Remember that ripple in the history/future that Shaarvan and Thal spoke of? I have seen it. It is real. It is a pathway of choices, like a trail of stones placed in the sand. One must position each foot on the stone that will best serve to carry one forward. But there is no way to move backward on that path. The stones behind each step disappear into history. One can only advance on the ripples of time.

"I can see across some of those ripples. Shaarvan is there. Our paths cross many times. He will take me back, Tren. But I cannot see when. Time has no meaning on that path. It could be Passes or Tides — it is all the same to the Future."

"Then you have won."

"No one ever wins. One only does the best one can not to slip between the stones."

"What does that mean — to slip between the stones? What would happen then?"

Tren took a step toward me, his face intense with questions. Worry had become prominent feature in his eyes.

"I don't know. That is what I can't see. The ripples of the future, of time, only allow for certain sights. As the ripples move (they are always moving, Tren, like a sheet hung outside, buckling in the wind), other visions are given. Perhaps there are stones beneath the path, and it is simply that I cannot see them. Possibly, to fall off the path would mean death, rebirth, or the Shapechanger view of a different plane of existence. The candle did not tell me everything, Tren."

"But you are wiser."

"I see more, but I am the same."

He nodded. "Do you see how I feel about you? Do the ripples tell you that?"

I looked down. Of course, I knew he loved me, but I could not deal with that at the moment.

"I must exchange this gown for a fresh one. You may stay or leave, as it pleases you, Tren."

"What pleases you? That I stay, or that I go?"

"I would like you to stay, but I cannot offer you more. I am a Priestess, but I am first a woman whose husband has left her. I will conquer Thenos. Then, I will grieve, Tren."

Tren smiled and nodded his head. "I understand. I shall wait."

I showered and did my hair as elaborately as I could without the flowers, I would have preferred. I did not bother covering up when I came out. Tren had seen me before. My dress was simple, white for the innocence that Thenos always spoke of. I hoped it would please him.

"What do you think, Tren?" I asked him, twirling around when I was ready.

"If I were Shaarvan, I would stick around."

We walked out together and headed for the Control Room. The others were glued to the sight of Thenos' ship growing closer on the screen.

"Speedy recovery, Wife. Did Tren service your needs, or do you expect Thenos to handle those?"

Spelon growled and went for Shaarvan.

"No," I commanded. "He is my husband. But like Thal, his jealousy eats at his wisdom. Lock him up."

It took both Spelon and Tenor to subdue Shaarvan. It was Thedar's fist that ended the struggle. I ordered Spelon to stay with me and Tenor and Thedar to go guard Shaarvan. Tren, I asked to watch over the babies. Thal had, at some point, already slipped away, back to his studies.

Spelon handed me the shortpipe. I didn't know where to put it. My dress had no pockets. I placed it down on a chair and folded one of Thandar's baby blankets over it.

"Leave now, Spelon. It is time."

Spelon went down on his knees and kissed my hand. "It is not right for me to leave you unchaperoned with Thenos. I shall give my life for you."

I shook my head. I reached out and touched his face. "Your life is too precious to me for you to give it away meaninglessly. I command that you leave."

He bowed his head. "Priestess," he acknowledged my new position. "I shall serve you always. Know that my heart goes with you, High Priestess Shaara."

"I know, Spelon."

The door closing behind his exit was such an empty sound. Only the high-pitched squeak of Thenos' ship mounting ours, its metal scratching metal, sounded as sad.

I called Thenos then. *"I have guards on Shaarvan. He will not disturb us. Come to me. I am ready now."*

*"You do not know what **ready** means, my virgin."*

"I know what it is to hunger when a voice calls me in the night. I know what it means to be taken further away from the sweet words that sang to me."

"Stars in Heaven! Your voice plays music to me. Who guards you now?"

"I am alone. They are all busy."

"I am coming."

"Thenos, I am afraid."

"Of me?"

"Will you be gentle with me?"

"Surely you jest."

"Please."

*"Shaara, you are **too** innocent."*

"Do you love me?"

"I am transferring to your ship now."

"Do you love me?"

"Shaara, I shall try to be gentle."

"You will not hurt me?"

"You ask too much of me."

"Do you love me?"

"I am almost there with you."

"But I am frightened that you will hurt me."

"Do you not understand that I must?"

"Do you love me?"

"Stop asking that."

"I cannot love you unless you love me."

"I am here," he said, and he stood before me. His body had aged. He was no longer a youth but a male fully grown into his Power.

He stood a moment, staring at me. His guards came towards me, and I screamed. "No, they frighten me, Thenos."

He waved them back.

"You are more beautiful, Shaara, than you were when I first saw you."

I stared at the ground as if shy.

"Check her," Thenos said.

The guards again started towards me.

"Thenos, please don't let them touch me. I want only you to . . ." Again, I stopped as if I could not go on.

"I am hard for you, Shaara, but I am not a fool."

"I have a shortpipe, but it is not on me. I shall tell you where it is if you promise to be gentle with me."

"I promise."

"It's on the chair. They made me take it in case you came for me. They told me to kill myself and never let you near me. I was supposed to stay in my room, but you understand, don't you, Thenos? I had to see you."

The guards found the shortpipe and took it. They stood ready to search me at the word of Thenos, but he was too busy listening to me. He waved them on.

"Thenos, you do not trust me?" I cried. "You will make them touch me?"

Thenos nodded for the guards to search me. They moved closer.

"Wait," I said.

Thenos flashed a hand signal, and the guards stopped.

"If I prove to you that I have no weapons on me, are you going to . . ." I pretended I could not say the words. "Not with them watching . . ."

"If they find no weapons on you, they will return to the ship while we are busy."

"Thank you, Thenos. I shall take off my dress so you can see. Could they look away, please, Thenos?"

I was projecting like crazy. The guards were convinced I was as innocent as a newly stolen girl. Thenos was suspicious, but he was weakening. As I pulled up my dress slowly, he waved the guards away.

"Stars! You are perfect. I have looked forward to this day for two Passes, my princess."

"But you will be . . ."

"Enough of that! I shall take you as a Shapechanger should take a woman — with violence and lust. You are mine, Thenosa."

Thenos took two steps forward, and his hand reached out. I was surprised he had no skill. The hand that squeezed my breast was only painful. It held no Power of the Web.

"Oh, Thenos. I knew you would be like this. I feel your lust."

He pressed his body full against me, ramming his torso into me like he was a goat fighting a fence post.

"Oh, please, kiss me, Thenos, now . . ."

As if I'd issued an invitation he'd been waiting for, his mouth ground into mine. His tongue was a goldfish, slimy and cold. I concentrated extra hard on showing how much I savored his kiss.

His hands were pinching at my breasts. He seemed to think that it was necessary to make my nipples hard.

"Yes," I cried out as if I were ecstatic. "Oh, yes!"

I moaned loudly and searched through Thenos' mind. I disconnected his speech first. He never felt it. His goldfish was almost gagging me. Next was his muscle control, snip, snip. Thenos' body was heavier than I'd thought it would be. I couldn't support him. He sagged and fell to the ground. A pool of urine collected around his ramming tool.

I left him there and called for Spelon. I knew he'd waited at the door. He rushed in instantly.

"Get Shaarvan if he's conscious. Let's see what kind of military plans you males can pull from Thenos' brain."

I pulled on my dress and sat down to wait. I was tired, but the shock of what I'd done had not yet hit me. I was still angry with Thenos and the way his hands had brutalized my body.

Shaarvan, when he came in, didn't meet my eyes. He bent over his brother and began to read through his thoughts. Each of the bondmates took their turn and pulled out what they wanted. When they finished and stood watching me, I turned to Shaarvan.

"I can kill him, my husband, or you can. I obey your command."

Shaarvan looked deeply into my eyes. I thought for that one brief moment I had seen our history wrong. Shaarvan would kill Thenos, and he would still be my husband, and we could go on as before . . . But then he turned from me.

"It is your kill, High Priestess. You have won."

My mind sifted possibilities, looking for another path, but there was no stone that would lead me where I wanted to go. One of the males could kill Thenos, but it would not change Shaarvan's mind. I could leave Thenos as a vegetable, but that was cruel and would serve no purpose. With a shrug, I looked back at Thenos. I searched inside his brain and cut the final cord.

He gasped once, and it was over. Thenos would blow up no more nurseries.

"Now, my lord?" I asked.

"Now, out of my way, woman, and preferably, out of my sight."

Spelon

When the death of Thenos was made known to his ship, like cowards, his crew of commoners fled. We did not chase them. I was eager to shoot a cannon across their bow, but Shaarvan's decision was to let them go.

I think he was in shock. We should not have listened to him. But he was Shaarvan, a Trendacons, General of Altar's Military, so we bowed to his ruling in the matter.

235

What I could not abide was his decision concerning the High Priestess. Shaarvan was a fool to turn away from her. I could not forgive him for that. He wounded her gravely.

Tren

I do not understand Shaarvan at all. His wife just solved his biggest problem, and he refused to thank her *or* forgive her. She cried and begged sweetly for his pardon. She promised to revoke her Priestesshood. But he refused to speak to her.

In fact, he treated her as if she were an abomination. He scorned her tears and derided whatever she said. I spoke up for Shaara, as did the others, but it did no good. She only heard Shaarvan. I hated watching her wilt from her guilt.

Worst of all, Shaarvan forbade her being with her sons. How dare he castigate her so cruelly! She saved the lives of her children, but Shaarvan does not want to see it. He has turned cold and hardhearted.

He told us that he was returning to Altar. Of course, we knew that he would depart — but not without Shaara. We were sick over it. Every one of us ignored the noninterference rule of the Shapechanger and attempted to talk some sense into Shaarvan's stubborn head, but he refused to listen.

How could he do this to Shaara? How could he be so ruthless?

He told us that she belonged to Westla now. Yes, we would take her there. But I do not think she wants to go.

Shaarvan said that she was free from him. She was a Priestess and henceforth must choose her own path.

Why did Shaarvan not see what is clear to us — that Shaara only wants to be his wife? My brother is a fool. How can he leave her like this? How can he refuse to take her back?

I was set to go with the others, with Shaara, but Shaarvan said that the Trendacons must meet me. So, I have to leave my love again. I suppose that means I will be involved with the war, although the battle has mainly been ended by Shaara killing Thenos. At least, we hope so.

I would have argued, wishing to stay near Shaara and my friends, but I remembered what Tessa had said. Shaarvan needed me. I must help him find a new route.

Her bondmates promised to stay with the children (and Shaara.) Shaarvan declared that Shaara no longer needed them, He didn't seem to care if they watched over her or not, although he did insist they turn Thal over to the Agency of the Troubled.

Then Shaarvan told us he would send for his sons when it was safe. Again no mention of his wife. Poor Shaara. She is devastated.

His lack of concern for Shaara disgusted Spelon, who took a moment to send a deep, thrust fist into Shaarvan's face — a well-deserved fist, if you ask me. Thedar, Tenor, and I were strangely silent. None of us contested the punch. (In fact, I felt the urge to join in with Spelon. Maybe they did, too.)

The bond we feel for Shaara is great. We love her. We regret the way things are being left. None of us will turn against her. How can Shaarvan?

Chapter Seven

Shaara

So, the history books will tell you that the Priestess Shaara killed the dreaded tyrant of Altar. And, soon, you will be able to read how Shaarvan ended the battles of the war-torn land and how peace ruled in Altar once again (I hope.)

But history books never tell you the important parts — the parts significant to a woman anyway. Who suffered, how did they endure, what did they do after, where did they go, and how did each character continue with his (or her) life? Those are the questions the history books should *really* tell us.

Maybe that's the difference between a good story and a history book. A good story ties up the ends beautifully. But dry records of fact are just a series of beginnings and endings without any middle, and the middle is where all the good stuff lies. Mostly.

Good stories have happy endings. The hero triumphs and the heroine cries her happy tears, and we all feel good. Yet, I'm sure it never works that way in nonfictional accounts. Does anyone ever *feel* anything inside a history book? After they look around and see the dead, the deceived, and the deserted.

Always, if I have a choice, I prefer a good story. But, although we know the beginning and the middle of this one, with all its juicy stuff, I guess we can leave the ending for the future. After all, who wants to read about how the hero flew off and the heroine just persevered, trudging on alone?

~~~~~~

The trip back to Westla was uneventful. I didn't retreat to the snow. That was a coward's way of dealing with life. I realize that now. Even a Priestess has goals to strive for, children to care for, Shapechanger guardians who love me.

I worked out with Spelon and the others daily. I continued to ignore Thal, who mainly stayed in his rooms, and I played with the children, sometimes sneaking in to hear their lessons. Shaarvan had ordered that I was to have no contact with the children, but none of my guardians obeyed that. Besides, by Shaarvan's own words, I was no longer under his authority.

My bondsmen rarely chided me for anything after the candle lighting. No more obeying, being silent, licking the floor all around their boots. (Okay, the last might have been a bit of an exaggeration, but Tessa would have approved of my sarcasm.) I'd earned my freedom and my liberation from the males' tyranny.

Spelon was still the one in charge, not of me, perhaps, but of the group. It would have been his right to bed me, but although he crept into my room the second night after Shaarvan's departure, he did not climb into my bed but merely stretched out on the floor beside me. I ignored his presence for three Tides before I insisted that he join me in my bed.

And then, for many nights, my very patient bondsman — I suppose now my Second Husband, although I was unsure of titles anymore — held me in his arms and did not ask for more.

But Shapechanger females are engineered to require the attention of a male. I soon dissolved into need, and Spelon ended my torture. He did not web me. He asked. What a pleasant surprise.

Thedar, Tenor, and Spelon, even without the responsibility of guarding me, continued to be what I guess one could call my friends. They never turned away from me as Shaarvan had. I was thankful for that, for their continued support, and because none of them said, "I told you so."

And Thal's ship sped us forward.

We stopped twice for supplies. No agents of Altar attempted to storm our ship in search of the children or for me. Perhaps that is all behind us. We hope. But I did not leave the ship. "Precautions are always wise," as Tenor said.

Spelon stayed with me, Thedar attended the children, and Thal and Tenor made their way through the bureaucracy of port etiquette. Tenor said that Thal acted sane throughout their stay. For such short periods of time, he seems himself, but then he lapses back into the belief that I am still his. Keeping him away from me makes him calmer. He has not yet asked to see the children. I am not sure he remembers them.

A little more than a halfPass brought us finally to Westla. From a distance, the artificial station is planet-like, rounded, and shaded as if continents and oceans form its structure. But as one nears, the framework of its outer surface resembles metal more than landmass.

Spiderweb-like black walls seem to segment it into portions. Some areas are agricultural, although most plants are raised in greenhouse domes that intensify the faint solar rays from the star too far away to produce sufficient light energy. (Tenor told me that solar space modules capture the primary energy needs of Westla.)

As we enter the proximity zone, we can see the sections of the planet that are natural landscapes and parks for everything from skiing to water sports. In other words, all the diversity of a normal planet is found in this one manufactured orb that contains millions of Shapechanger.

It is rather amazing, but somehow, for me, claustrophobic, although I must admit that the trees on Westla are every bit as real as those found on Earth. The smells and textures, even the pinecones that fall, are the same as in my home world, and Westla's air never smells stale or insufficient, so the claustrophobia, as Shaarvan used to call it, is all in my mind. (But isn't that what claustrophobia is?)

As our ship comes closer, the capital city of West, where Tem and most of the officials are quartered, is more clearly visible. It contains the largest percentage of inhabitants and is where I used to live with Shaarvan and later with Thal. The Priestess training facilities are also near there, Tenor tells me. Space Port West, where we'll be landing, is only for residents. Although we've been gone a long time, I guess that's what we are — or will be (again).

We can see the tiger's eye now through our ship's window. It once frightened me. I thought it was the eye of a great beast. But all the beasts of Westla are manlike except when they Shapechange into Saberey. Whoops, that includes me, too, now. I can Shapechange just as skillfully as a male.

We enter through the eye, plummeting downward. No more fear of falling. I have faith in the computers onboard the ship. They have expertly landed us on many planets. My fears are no longer shipbound but of the future. I think I will be paving a new path. No other female has attained Priesthood at my age nor was married and deserted. Tessa will cackle ceaselessly at that. Maybe I will one day, too.

But for right now, all I can do is walk the path of stones and review the beginnings of my adventure in these new worlds.

I once was Terran, then Altarian, then Shapechanger. I have been a slave on Freinanan and Seconded on Deadstar. I am a Westlan High Priestess. I am all these women and more, but the most important thing is that I still love my husband. But yet, for a while, I am no longer Shaara of Shaarvan.

The Shaarvan Series Continues With:

Book Seven Shaara, Priestess of Westla